MW01016213

The Legend of Walt the Wizard

Tait Ressler (signature)

Tait Ressler

authorHOUSE®

AuthorHouse™
1663 Liberty Drive
Bloomington, IN 47403
www.authorhouse.com
Phone: 1-800-839-8640

First published by AuthorHouse 2/8/2010

ISBN: 978-1-4490-6663-5 (sc)

Printed in the United States of America
Bloomington, Indiana

This book is printed on acid-free paper.

To: My Dad Don for always believing in me and helping my dream become a reality.
My Mom Sharon who encouraged me to begin reading at a young age.
My Brothers Austin and Tyler, who are willing to help when I need them.
Lastly to Sue Skalicky, for showing me my gift as a writer and for being my biggest fan.

Chapter 1
Secrets

It was a warm summer morning in the big city of London. Cars were zooming around on every street and stores were just beginning to open. It seemed like everybody was as happy and alive as ever, but there was one person still at home in a warm, soft bed sound asleep with dreams filling his head. He didn't like mornings. He preferred midday when there weren't so many people out and it wasn't so busy.

Walt's mother left early for work most mornings. By the time the boy awakened, the house was quiet and the sun was high overhead. On weekdays, Walt's dad wasn't around much either. He owned a travel agency and often stayed there all night booking international trips for business people from around the globe.

Walt finally stumbled out of bed bleary-eyed and yawning. By this time it was late in the afternoon. He took a quick shower, dressed, and headed out to see what new adventures awaited him. During the summer, Walt was free to do what he liked until his mother got off work. London held thousands of places a young lad could explore, all within easy reach of the famous "Tube." On his own, he spent hours at the British National Museum, The Victoria and Albert Museum and The Tower of London. He even took in the occasional matinee in the theatre district near Leicester Square. Today, though, Walt had something else in mind. Perhaps a trip to the East End or to what Walt called "The Haunted East End." He'd poke around its narrow streets and explore some of the old churches he'd seen. Then, he would head home for supper.

Walt turned a corner on his way to Victoria station when his father, Joseph, pulled up beside him in his shiny black convertible.

"Hello, Walt," his father called. "Have you made urgent plans for today?"

Walt wondered why his father was not working. "Nothing cast in stone," Walt responded. "Why do you want to know?"

His father said, "Well, I was hoping you would have lunch with me. Can you spare your old dad the time?"

"Sure," Walt said and got in the car. "Why aren't you at the office?"

"I took the day o f f "

Walt was surprised. The only time Walt could remember his father taking a day off was when the Queen Mum passed away a few years back.

"Where should we eat?" Joe asked Walt.

"Remember that quaint old restaurant with the huge fish sign," said Walt. "We never go there anymore."

The local establishment had the best fish and chips in London, even though the exterior of the building was unremarkable. The only indication of the business inside was a huge turquoise and gold fish hanging above the entrance. In fact, the restaurant didn't even have a name. What it did have was a loyal following among connoisseurs of fish.

"Okay then, off we go to the fish house!" Joe exclaimed. Walt and Joe arrived at the restaurant at one o'clock. The lunch crowd had thinned so it wasn't too busy.

Walt and his father made their way to a table by a window and sat down.

"So, what have you been doing all day besides driving around and not going to work?" Walt asked his father.

"I went to see your grandfather today and then I went to the bank."

"You went to see Grandfather? Why haven't I seen or met any of my relatives and why haven't I gone to see my grandparents?"

"Well," his dad replied, "they don't all live here."

"My grandfather must live in London because you went to see him today, right?"

"Yes," Joe answered his son. "Your grandfather does live in the city, but if you met him you might think he is a bit odd. The reason I saw him today is because he had a present he wanted me to give you."

Walt's father pulled a small black silk bag from his pants pocket and pushed it across the table to Walt. Walt stared at it thoughtfully.

"Don't you want to know what's inside?" Joe asked.

Walt nodded. He carefully untied the gold strings that closed the bag. He reached into the silk bag, feeling an unusual shape. Walt's jaw dropped as he pulled out a beautiful blue sapphire medallion.

"What is this?" he asked a quizzical look on his face.

"It's a medallion and it belonged to your grandfather," Joe said. "According to your grandfather when he created it he infused magical power into it."

"What does it do?"

"Walt," his father interrupted him. "You may not believe me but your grandfather is a wizard. He is the wizard Merlin to be exact."

Walt's mouth fell open again. "What? That can't be! How? I thought Merlin only existed in books or fairy tales."

"I probably shouldn't have told you. I knew it would come as a surprise and be difficult for you to understand."

"Why didn't you tell me sooner?" Walt asked with anger in his voice. He was upset that his father thought he was too young or to close-minded to understand

"I wanted to wait until the right time."

"So you think this is the right time?" Walt was nearly yelling at his father. It was a reaction his father had not anticipated.

"Walt! Quiet! Someone might hear you. I know you're upset and you have every right to be. I really wanted to tell you sooner. But your mother would not allow it."

"Don't you think I had a right to know?" Walt demanded. "Why would mum even care anyways? He is my grandfather after all." Walt was beginning to regain control. "So what do you think she's going to say when she finds out I know?"

"That's a bit of a problem," Joe said. "You must not let your mother find out. Not a word will be said. Do you understand me?

Walt nodded.

"If your mum knew I told you she would never forgive me. Promise me you will not tell anyone, not even your friends!" Walt's father pleaded.

"Okay. I won't breathe a word," Walt agreed. "But she's bound to find out sooner or later."

"I know that, but for now not a word."

"Okay," Walt said again. "

For now just know that your grandfather loves you and wanted you to have his medallion. The rest will be explained at the right time. Joe picked up the ticket and rose from the table. "Oh, one more thing, don't forget to put that medallion somewhere safe and somewhere where your mother won't find it."

They left the restaurant and Walt still had no understanding of the magic of the Medallion. He knew nothing more about his grandfather other than that he was a great wizard and that his grandfather loved him. Walt felt he had a lot more questions than answers.

Chapter 2
An Unexpected Guest

It had been a week since Walt's dad had given him the medallion and he still hadn't figured out what kind of magic it held. He wished there was someone he could ask but his father had only given him cryptic replies.

"Mum doesn't know I have it, and that's a good thing," Walt thought to himself as he slipped the medallion around his neck like a necklace. The medallion had a metal chain attached to it through a tiny adornment at the top; this made its use more convenient ensuring that the owner would not lose it so easily.

At dinner that evening they had an unexpected guest. Walt's mum wasn't too happy, but rather than spoiling the whole thing let's start the story from the beginning.

It all began when they sat down for dinner. Dad was talking about how many phone calls he had gotten at work. Mum talked about what a rough day she had at her office. Then it happened, a knock on the door. Walt's father left the table to answer it and when he returned he was with an old man who was very tall and stood very straight. The gentleman had a long beard and gold-rimmed glasses that he wore on the tip of his nose.

Walt's Mum looked surprised that they had the guest, especially at such a late hour.

"Hello," she said trying to look calm, but she was obviously uncomfortable.

"Hello, Jane," the man said. "How are you?" he added kindly.

"I'm well. Please, have a seat. I'm sorry I didn't set another place at the table. I thought you had decided not to come," she said looking embarrassed.

"I apologize, my dear. I've always had trouble with modern devices. I tried to call to confirm, but I just got my first cell phone and I couldn't figure out how to use the piece of rubbish."

Dad sat back down while Walt's mum went to the kitchen. She returned with a plate of food for their guest. The old man sat beside Walt. Walt thought it was strange that this old man who knew all of their names was in their house when Walt had no idea who the visitor was.

"Walt, your mum and I didn't know if this would be a good time to introduce your grandfather but we thought if he came to the house ..."

Walt interrupted him. "What are you saying?" Walt yelled so loud at his father that he almost choked on his meat. "You're telling me this man beside me is my grandfather. You didn't even tell me he was coming."

"Yes, Walt. We're sorry we didn't tell you sooner," said Mum apologetically.

"Oh, so you both kept secrets from me. How long were you going to let this go on? Let me tell you both something. I'm fifteen years old. I will be growing up faster now!" Walt shouted.

"What are you talking about?" Mum said looking at Walt like she was about to lose her calm

Everybody got quiet. Then Walt realized what he had just done and he felt horrible for yelling at his parents. He was about to tell everyone that he had the medallion but his mother still didn't know he had it. The only thing he could do now was change the subject. So, Walt asked his grandfather, "Why haven't I met you before?"

"Well, Walter, we have met," said Merlin. I haven't seen you in a very long time and you probably don't remember."

"Walt," Mum inserted, "I want to know the other secret we were keeping from you now."

"Jane don't fluster the boy," said Joe.

Walt's mother was becoming very impatient with both Walt and his father but before she was able to say another word Joe spoke up.

"Jane, he knows about the medallion. I gave it to him when we went to lunch last week." Joe looked at her for a few moments in silence.

"Smashing, "Jane replied sarcastically.

"He has a right to know, Jane."

"Why now?"

`Because he's fifteen and his powers have already started developing even though Walt doesn't know it. Without a guiding hand, it could be disastrous.

"Dad," Joe turned to Merlin. "He also knows about you. So, I guess it's time to start his training."

Chapter 3
Walt's Magical Beginning

Even though it was a Saturday Walt awoke early. Usually both his parents were home leisurely enjoying their Saturday morning in bed. About ten, Mum would fix a brunch and then she would tend her garden. This morning Walt's dad was dressed and watching the morning news while surprisingly his mum was gone. Walt wondered where she was.

"Dad," Walt asked. "Where's mum? She's not in the house."

"Walt don't bother looking. She left and went to her mother's. She's a little upset with me at the moment. No need to worry. She'll cool off and things will return to normal," Joe said confidently.

"Why are you up so early?"

"This morning I went to see your grandfather. He will be doing your training as a wizard."

"Training as a wizard?" Walt asked.

"I don't know when exactly," Joe said. "Your grandfather said he had things to attend to this afternoon. When he is finished he will come by for you."

"But dad why can't you train me?" Walt asked. "I would rather have you do it instead because I don't know grandfather."

"Walt I know you would rather I train you but your grandfather has more skills in magic then any wizard I know. Besides, I left most of my wizard skills behind when I married your Mum on the condition that your grandfather could pass my birthright onto you. So please do this for your Mum and I okay?"

"Oh alright" Walt, answered back.

"Good. I almost forgot to give you this. It's from your grandfather." Walt's father gave him an envelope addressed to him.

"Well go ahead open it" his father said. Walt stood staring at the letter for a few seconds bewildered, wondering if he should open it or not.

"Okay Walt finally said here I go."

He slowly opened it trying not to rip it. Walt took out a piece of paper, unfolded it. He read the writing on it very clearly aloud so his father could hear.

"It says:

`Dear Walt

It's me your grandfather I was just writing to tell you that you are welcome to come to my academy to be trained in magic. But note this you won't be the only one to attend there will be other teenagers there too so don't worry. This is entirely your choice, so if you choose not to come I will understand.

Sincerely yours always,

Merlin

P.S. If you're planning to attend, tell me this evening. Merlin's Academy of Magic."

Walt felt his insides jump for joy. He was really going to be a wizard and learn powerful spells and be with others like himself. "I'm ready to become what I was born to be."

His father turned to him, smiled and said, "Good. I'm glad for you." Walt looked at the clock. He turned back to his father and asked.

"When is he coming then?"

Joe turned to Walt and was about to tell him when there was a knock on the door.

"Oh," he said, "that must be him." Then they stared at each other for a moment.

Chapter 4
Walt's First Magic Lesson

Walt ran to the door his heart pounding as he went, curious about what his first lesson might be and what he would learn with his grandfather.

He opened the door to find Merlin in clothing much better looking than the last time he had seen him.

"Well, well, well," Merlin said as he stood in the doorway. "Are you ready?" he asked in an excited tone of voice.

"Well," said Walt, "what will we be doing?" Walt asked curiously.

"We have to get you some training if you're going to come to my academy. That is if you want to?" he said looking Walt right in the eyes.

"Yes. I want to come," Walt said with excitement in his voice.

"Well, let's be on our way then. Bye Joe," Merlin said to Walt's dad when they left the house. They walked down the path and down the street then suddenly came to the back of an alley a few blocks down from Walt's house.

"All right, my boy," said Merlin "The reason we stopped here is I want to make sure you truly want to do this. You know if you don't, we're wasting our time."

"Okay," Walt interjected. "I've told you I truly want to do this, so why do you keep asking me?"

Merlin looked at Walt and said, "I know you don't know me very well."

"It's a little strange for me," Walt said. "I just didn't know

about being a wizard until now but I trust you, Grandfather." They began walking again and came to a more private area. Merlin asked Walt, "Are you wearing the medallion?" "Yeah," said Walt.

He had been wearing it ever since his father gave it to him at the fish house. Walt was surprised his mum hadn't noticed he had the medallion yet.

"Why? What are we going to do with it?" Walt asked.

"Well," Merlin said. "First I'll teach you how to defend yourself against a curse. Don't worry this won't hurt you in any way you might just get knocked down."

Walt stood there wondering how he would defend himself without a wand.

"Grandfather?" Walt asked.

Merlin turned to Walt seeing that there was concern in his eyes. "Yes, what is it?"

"I don't have a wand," he said looking sadly at the ground. "Don't worry, my boy. I brought one for you." Merlin replied.

Walt looked excitedly at his grandfather. Merlin handed him a black wooden wand.

"Thank you," Walt said with admiration.

"Now I want you to repeat after me: *Abracadabra Alacazam Invisious Disappearo*"

Walt repeated the spell and pointed his new wand at a tree. All of sudden it disappeared.

Walt rubbed his eyes to make sure what he had seen was real.

Merlin smiled at him and said, "Okay. You just passed your first lesson for tonight."

Walt turned to Merlin. "Aren't you going to teach me any more tonight? Aren't you going to show me how to be more powerful? I thought you said we would go over many things, not just one spell," Walt ended.

"Walt, what I meant is that we would go over some things such as the world of wizardry not just spells. We will go over more things. Don't worry that you're not learning more magic yet. You have to understand that it will take more time than just one night." Merlin became quiet as they walked back to Walt's house.

Chapter 5
Walt's Tour of the Academy

"Guess what!" Walt yelled as he returned home a few weeks later. "I have experienced my first magic lesson with grandfather."

"What?" called his mother from her room.

"I cast my first spell a few weeks ago," he said excitedly. His mum was now home again from her mother's. Walt wondered why she had left in the first place.

"Well, good for you dear. What's he going to teach you next?" she asked.

"I don't know he just told me we would meet again another night. I don't really know when though."

"Oh," she replied. His mother was now accepting the fact that Walt knew he was a wizard which Walt liked a lot.

"I think he might be coming again tonight to show me the academy," he told his mother.

"Well, your father and I are going out tonight so you'll be home alone until your grandfather arrives to pick you up." "All right," Walt replied. He suddenly had an idea. "Mum, can I talk to you?"

"Sure," she said. "What is it?"

"I was wondering if you are a witch?" Walt felt embarrassed asking such a strange question, but he had and he wanted to know. How could he be related to Merlin without knowing if both his parents were magic.

His mother hesitated a while and said, "Yes, I am. But Merlin is your father's father. Understand now?"

"Yes, that's understandable." All of a sudden there was a knock on the door. "I'll get it," said Walt. He strode to the door not expecting Merlin to be there smiling.

"Hello, Walt. Shall we be going? I'm sorry for being so early but we must be going a little earlier tonight. We've lots to do."

"Okay," said Walt not yet noticing the girl standing next to Merlin.

"Good bye, Jane," said Merlin as they left. They walked at a brisk pace heading down the street. "Walt," said his grandfather stopping. "I'd like you to meet Elza." Merlin placed a gentle hand on the girl's shoulder.

Walt noticed the pretty young lady and said "hello" blushing.

"Now that we've gotten that out of the way we will be going to the academy tonight for a tour. The reason why I'm taking you both is because I want to train both of you to become my apprentices." Walt was overjoyed by this and Elza smiled happily.

They were now heading into open country. They suddenly stopped when Merlin said "Walt, grab my hand. Elza take Walt's hand and hold on tight." Elza moved towards Walt and held out her hand. Walt grabbed it shyly. Merlin said a spell Walt couldn't understand and suddenly they zipped off the ground and flew into the air. Then everything was pitch black. Walt had trouble knowing where he was. He shouted,

"Where are we going now?" Then before he could get an answer everything became light again and they were heading toward the ground. They landed and Walt and Elza looked up to see a huge castle with a lowered drawbridge in front of them. Huge maple doors opened silently as they walked across the bridge.

Merlin then said, "Welcome to M.A.M. or Merlin's Academy of Magic," he said proudly. They entered. Walt and Elza looked all around, their eyes wide with surprise.

"Now," said Merlin. "I am the headmaster of this academy. As my students you will both learn all that I and my fellow professors can teach you. There will be other students your age soon coming here too, so you will not be the only ones."

As they walked Merlin told them about the many things they would learn while attending school at the fine castle. They were amazed at what Merlin told them and they were astounded by the beauty of the academy.

Finishing their tour Merlin said, "Your first day of class will begin on August first of this year," They headed back towards the big maple doors. Then they left the academy. As Merlin and Walt walked back to Walt's house after dropping Elza off at her house, Walt's mind was spinning. Then Merlin left.

Walt stood in the doorway soon his mind returned to normal and he could only think of one thing and one thing only, realizing that he was in love with Elza even though they had exchanged only a few words in the even fewer hours they had spent together.

Chapter 6
A Very Evil Enemy

Walt continued to train with Merlin and Elza every evening learning more spells and becoming stronger as each evening passed.

Walt also continued to dream of Elza. After dropping her off at her house each evening he would happily think about the events of the day and his time with her. He was surprised his parents and Merlin hadn't found out about his feelings for Elza. He also was afraid to confront Elza with his feelings for her. "I have to tell her tonight," he told himself. Walt then headed to his room deciding to practice some of the spells he had learned.

After reviewing incantations for awhile, he stepped outside and into the backyard. His parents were still at work so he was home alone once again. *"Abracadabra Alacazam Invisious*

Disappearo," he said aiming his wand at his hand. He was shocked when he looked again at his hand and found it was now transparent. "I didn't know I could make myself disappear," Walt yelled with joy.

Suddenly he heard someone say, "Bravo, young man," Walt quickly spun around seeing an older man standing in the backyard. "Who are you and what are you doing here?" he asked white-faced.

"Oh don't worry. Let's just say I'm a family friend," he said staring Walt right in the eyes. Walt was immediately ill at ease.

"You better leave before I curse you!" Walt shouted at him. "Get out of here now and never come back," he shouted. "I just want to.."

"NO!" Walt ran at him and fell hard on the ground. "I know you're not a friend of my parents. Leave now or I'll kill you!" he yelled.

"But young man, I just want to see how your medallion works," he pleaded.

"How do you know I have a medallion?" Walt asked. "Well I can't tell you that," the man said sounding scared. "Fine," Walt said, "take this *Flameo Ascendo*, "aiming his wand at the ground and suddenly flames came shooting straight into the air finding their target and chasing after the man. The man ran away in fright.

Unnerved, Walt looked at his watch and decided to head back inside and get ready for practice. He checked every corner of his house to make sure the old man was gone. He was, so Walt got ready to go for their evening lesson. By that time there was a knock on the door. Walt went to the door and opened it. He was expecting Merlin and Elza together however it was just Elza staring him in the face.

"Ah ... hello," Walt said blushing, feeling a slight bit nervous and shy.

"Hi," said Elza back at him. "May I come in?" she asked politely.

"Uh, sure," said Walt expecting to leave for practice. "Are we going to train tonight?" Walt asked her.

"I'm not sure," said Elza looking at him.

"So why are you here?" said Walt.

"I'm bored," she said smiling. "Why are you so curious?" she wondered.

"Well you may not feel the same," Walt said. "I like you a lot." He then turned beet red

"I know we've only known each other for a couple of days so I feel a little awkward but I can't stop thinking about you."

Chapter 7
The First Day at the Academy

Walt awoke after a very wonderful dream, at least he thought.

"Walt," his mother called from downstairs. "You need to gather your things. Your grandfather will be here any minute to leave for the academy."

"All right," Walt called back."

He wasn't expecting to leave right now although he was very excited as he gathered his things. He packed his clothes then shuffled down the stairs as things tumbled down after him. There was a knock at the door, Walt ran to it his heart leaping as he went.

"Hello Walter," Merlin said happily. "We must be going," he said. Elza is waiting for us."

On the way to Elza's, Walt asked lots of questions. He was really excited now that he had found out about being a wizard. "Grandfather," Walt said, "I really can't wait to go to the academy. How many other students will there be?"

"Well, Walt, I'm sorry but I don't know how many there will be. Elza tells me you two are very good friends. That's wonderful. Now, here we are," Merlin said. "Well ~ go get her." Merlin smiled at him as Walt went to the door.

Walt knocked on the door and it slowly creaked open. Elza was standing there in the doorway smiling at him. She was wearing a long white dress with blue edges. Walt thought she looked stunning.

"Hello, Walt," Elza said

"Hello, Elza, you look beautiful Walt whispered.

Elza grabbed Walt's hand. They walked with Merlin to the deserted area where they had previously flown into the air. Once again they were soaring up. Then they were engulfed in blackness and finally they were pitching back toward the ground. Landing, Walt looked up at the big maple doors of M.A.M. They were now thrown open with hundreds of students going in.

"Wow," Walt and Elza said together when they walked into the school.

"Well, I'll see you two later," Merlin said snapping his fingers and suddenly disappearing.

"Ladies and Gentlemen," said a woman's voice at the far end of the hall. "You will be assigned certain rooms with one roommate. Boys with boys and girls with girls. You may not agree with your room assignment, however the headmaster has carefully chosen a room and roommate that is just right for each of you. So, without further ado I will announce the pairs."

The woman went through the list very quickly and Walt never heard his name. Elza was called and she said goodbye to Walt and left.

Finally, Walt heard his name. The lady stopped suddenly and said, "Oh, so you're the headmaster's grandson? Well you'll be paired with ... let's see ... Tom." Walt left the huddle of people and was directed up the staircase.

Soon he was in his room, number nine hundred and fifty. "Hello," he said to Tom.

The boy looked up from his suitcase. He had long black hair and dark blue eyes he was a few years older than Walt and rather skinny, slender almost sticklike.

"Hello. Nice to meet you," Tom replied his back to Walt. Walt unpacked quietly and Tom silently stuck his nose into a book. Walt later went to see Elza. They talked about their roommates and they were beginning to realize that they were both happy to be in the castle together.

Chapter 8
Magic and More

Walt was on his way to class when he was abruptly stopped by Merlin.

"Hello, Walter. I need you to come with me," he said

"But Grandpa, I've got class now," Walt said. He was wondering why Merlin needed him now.

"Walt," Merlin said, "please don't call me grandpa on castle grounds. Please refer to me as Merlin or Headmaster. I would feel more comfortable that way. Okay?" he finished.

"Oh, all right sorry. Now, what do you need me for?"

"Walt don't worry. I'm taking you to meet someone. This person is going to help me train you and Elza. Be aware that I will take you and Elza out of the castle every week to train and your instructors will be notified. One minute," Merlin said. They stopped at a classroom and Merlin went in. Walt waited for a few minutes, Merlin soon came out.

"So what am I going to miss?" Walt asked.

"Well," professor Stumpels said, "you should read pages one through ten for tomorrow. But you'll be back in time for the rest of your classes."

They went to get Elza and left the castle.

"Now we need to go to the center of London. That's where your other instructor Mr. Hucklesbey is. He is a very good friend of mine and he will help train you two when I'm busy. Now I will teach you two how to fly without the assistance of a broomstick or dragon. Ready point your wands toward yourselves and repeat after me. *Soarous!*"

Suddenly they flew into the air. Everything went black and Walt could feel the wind slashing at his face. He looked around in the semi darkness and soon saw Elza at his side, her light brown hair blown back. He could see even through the gray black mist how beautiful she was.

They zoomed towards the ground and everything got clear again. Sounds of people filled the air. "Come!" Merlin shouted. "Quickly now!" they were being dragged through swarms of people. Minutes passed and they walked on and on for what seemed like hours. "Here we are," Merlin finally said and they came to a stop at an old looking pub.

"Hello Merlin." said a rich looking man,

"Oh," Merlin jumped and turned to him. "Edward," he said happily, "its been years." They shook hands joyously. "Walt, Elza I'd like you to meet Mr. Edward Hucklesbey."

"Hello," they said to him.

"What an honor! I can't wait to start my training with you," he said.

"Well, Edward, you don't need to start right away," Merlin said.

"Oh sure. I know that."

"Right now I'd just like you to meet them and get to know them more. Anyway come into the pub and have some drinks." So all four of them walked into the pub. They sat towards the back

and Hucklesbey went to get some drinks. He came back with four drinks and sat down beside Merlin

Walt looked around the pub suspiciously wondering why Merlin brought them here.

"Well now, we need to start by going over basics," said Hucklesbey. "I know that you, Merlin, have taught them quite a lot. So I'll give you both these *Magic and More* books," he finished.

Walt took a book and skimmed the text. He saw pictures of many famous wizards and witches in it.

"Why do we need these?" Elza asked looking at Mr. Hucklesbey.

"I just want to start teaching you about the important things throughout the history of wizards and witches before your time because some of the things they did will benefit both of you. It should help you understand how spell casting works. I think both Merlin and I agree on that," he said giving a bit of a smirk to Merlin.

Merlin sat sipping his brandy silently.

"Well we best be off," he said downing the last of his brandy. He stood up putting on his cloak, wobbling slightly due to the strong effect of the drink he had so quickly drained. "Thank you Ed," said Merlin shaking his hand firmly, then Walt and Elza followed him to the door of the pub.

"Thank you Mr. Hucklesbey," said Elza.

"Bye. See you next week," he said to them as they walked out the door.

Chapter 9
The Medallion's Magic Power

Walt was having a fascinating school year at the academy in the middle of December. He had so much work to do. It was only a couple more weeks until Christmas and he still hadn't figured out the medallion's power, so he decided to ask Merlin how it worked.

Walt wanted to buy Elza a present for Christmas and he knew he didn't have too much money. He began heading to Merlin's tower when he saw the man that had been in his backyard that day in the summer. Walt was wondering why he was here. Soon he made it to the door of Merlin's office. His grandfather called him in and everything seemed calm now that Walt was with his grandfather in his office.

"Be seated, Walt," he said. Walt sat in a big armchair.

"Headmaster, I want to know how to use the medallion? What powers if any does it hold? Am I going to need it to protect myself against something evil or what?" he asked.

"Now, Walt, the power of the medallion will come to you if it is called."

"But headmaster how do I call the power of the medallion?"

"When a source of evil or in particular someone evil is near the medallion will glow a blue color."

"But I don't get it. How will it protect me when I am in danger?"

"Walt as long as you keep that medallion around your neck you cannot be hurt by any evil magic, you must understand that Mr. Hucklesbey and I won't always be there for you so you have to trust me. I will say this, believe in the power of the medallion. Soon it will be your only hope."

"What do you mean my only hope?" Walt asked confused.

"I will talk to you again soon. Now go you have class."

"Grandfather I have a favor to ask. I really like this girl and I would like to by her something for the holiday but I'm a little short on money."

"I see well the funny thing is your father had the same problem when he first met your mother. So how much do you want?" he asked.

"I don't know She isn't just any girl. Elza is well you know."

"Ah so you like Elza do you? In that case here this should be enough." he handed Walt a fistful of coins he then put them in his pocket and stood up.

"Thank you. I'll pay you back as soon as I can," Walt replied.

"Oh don't worry," said Merlin. "Well bye then."

"Walt good luck and remember what I told you and never give up." He finished and Walt left.

Chapter 10
Elza's Birthday

The castle was full of good cheer on this wonderful Christmas morning, everyone couldn't wait to get home for the holiday. The students were allowed to leave each Christmas to spend the holiday with their families and were to come back at the beginning of the New Year in January.

Walt had finally bought Elza a Christmas present a beautiful heart pendant necklace.

"Walt." He turned to find Elza standing behind him. "Oh yes what is it?"

"I have a present for you," she said.

"I also have a present for you," Walt told her as he took the gift from his pocket. "Go ahead open it."

"You first," she said.

"Oh okay," he ripped the wrapping paper off the box and inside it held a gold harmonica with a black case. He pulled it out and saw a note in the case, so he took it out unfolded it and read it aloud.

"Happy Christmas, Walt. I hope you like it. I love it." "Elza, thank you. It's brilliant. Now open yours."

Elza opened her gift very quickly. Her eyes grew very large
as she pulled out the necklace. "Oh Walt its beautiful," she bent towards him and kissed him on the cheek. "Thank you so much," she said.

"Here, I'll help you put it on," Walt helped her put the necklace on. Then he walked her to the front maple wood doors of the castle to say goodbye.

"It looks beautiful on you," he said. Have a good holiday. Oh happy birthday as well," he said. "I'll buy you something for your birthday over the holiday and I'll give it to you when I see you again.

Bye. I love you," he shouted as he ran out the doors.

Chapter 11
A New Pet

W alt was helping his mother set the table when there was a knock on the door.

"I'll get it." He knew who would be there as he opened the door, and sure enough he was right.

Merlin was standing in the doorway with red and green Christmas robes on. "May I come in?" he asked.

"Of course, Grandfather," Walt said to him.

"It smells wonderful," said Merlin. "Oh yes Walt, when we open gifts I've got an extra special gift for you."

"Oh, all right," then Walt strode back to the dining room. "Mum, is anyone else coming over?" he asked.

"Yes. Your father has invited the Henderson's over to open gifts and for supper. They're bringing their daughter. She's about your age. I think she may also go to the academy. Well she's not really their daughter. But your father told me that they are looking after her because her parents are traveling politicians or something," his mother finished.

"Do you know her name?"

"No, sorry dear. I don't," she answered.

Walt's mother finished setting the table and went to join the company.

The doorbell rang and Walt's father went answer it. "Walt," he called. "The Henderson's are here."

"Coming!" He answered back as he quietly walked out to the living room. "Walter, Mr. and Mrs. Henderson and I believe you may know this young lady." He said motioning toward a girl. He was shocked to see it was Elza.

"You must be Walter."

"Elza has told us so much about you," Mr. Henderson said smiling at him.

"Glad to meet you," said Walt. "We have had lots of fun at the academy," he replied. "Well, you two have fun now," they both said joining the rest of the company.

"I had no idea we were going to spend the holiday together," she told him."

"Neither did I," said Walt. "Want some punch?" he asked her. "No thanks, I'm fine," Elza replied as they made their way throughout the house. Walt's mother made her traditional chicken supper along with mashed potatoes, gravy, stuffing, corn, rice pudding and banana cream pie for desert.

Then after supper everyone gathered around the tree.

"Now," said Walt's father we would like to thank everyone for coming. It's been great and now it's time for presents.

Soon everyone had their presents and Walt remembered what Merlin had told him about the special gift.

"Grandpa," Walt said to Merlin reminding him about his surprise present, then Merlin went to get Walt's gift. "Here," he said and his jaw dropped open.

"But Grandpa, this is a baby dragon! My parents wouldn't allow it."

"Don't worry. They won't mind. I had a talk with them." "Thank you! What kind is it?" Walt asked him.

"He is a Golden Fire Tail, a rare species unknown to most wizards and witches, and he needs a name," he told Walt.

"I don't know ..." Walt thought for a moment,

" ... Ickaris, maybe. That's a good name," he said hugging Merlin. "Thanks, grandpa," he said happily.

Chapter 12
A Battle with the Enemy

Soon Ickaris grew. It was the middle of January now and Walt fed Ickaris every day. He ate whatever he could reach. So Walt had to keep a very close eye on him.

Walt wrote a letters to Elza every day. She had left London to visit her parents who had left the country because of meetings they had to attend in France for their jobs. Elza had decided to tag along because she hadn't seen them in a very long time.

Walt had seen the creepy man in his backyard again. His parents weren't home so he left a trap for the man this time.

There was a knock on the door, Walt ran to get it, was surprised to see Elza standing there smiling at him. "What are you doing here?" he asked.

"Well, I flew back alone," she said. "My parents stayed in France. They said I could come home, so I did because I wanted to spend some of the holiday with you." Walt invited Elza in and they talked about what they did with their time away from each other.

Then it happened. The front door blasted open and the creepy man that kept coming around Walt's house whenever he was alone stormed in.

"Well, well, well. Walter isn't it?" said the man. "Finally I've got you alone."

"Get out of my house," Walt demanded through clenched teeth, "or else."

"I just came to clear up a few things. First my name is Mandilus and the very powerful man I work for demands that I get your medallion. You don't know me but your father does.

Tell him I dropped by. Oh, and one more thing, your girlfriend is coming with me."

"No! stay away from her!" Walt had his wand drawn by now.

Both Elza and Walt crept toward the man who also had his wand drawn. He knew he was outnumbered so he slowly inched his way out the door. They were now outside it was windy and the snow was now melting due to the extensive heat wave that had swept the country. Elza was standing next to Walt with her wand out, they both were ready for anything.

"Now, now. I don't want to fight," said Mandilus. "I just want your medallion then I will leave."

"Constricto!" Walt shouted and a red string of light shot out of his wand. The man was thrown to the ground as the spell wrapped around his body. "Tell us why you're after my medallion?" Walt said to Mandilus who was now wrapped up in slime like sack. You could see the fear in his eyes as sweat dripped down his face.

"Never!" Said the man as the slime sack squeezed at his lungs and body.

"Have it your way then," said Walt, he and Elza drug the man into the cellar of Walt's house. "Send for my grandfather," Walt said as he tied the man up. "Who do you work for?" Walt asked the man his wand pointed at the man's skull.

The man was silent as Walt grew impatient.

The door flew open as Merlin came in with two men dressed in black. All of them had their wands drawn. Both Walt and Elza wondered how Merlin had gotten there so quickly. They however decided it wasn't important because he had arrived in time to help them.

"What's going on Walt?" Merlin demanded. Then all four men saw Mandilus in the cellar all tied up. "Take him away," Merlin ordered and the men shoved him up the stairs and out the house.

"Are you okay?" Merlin asked them both, they both nodded.

"Who is that man?" Elza asked Merlin shaking uncontrollably.

"Well he is a servant to one the worst dark wizards of our time. He thinks that by obtaining the medallion for his master they can eventually control all wizards and witches and take over my academy. Not to worry you're safe now. Walt I'll tell your parent's later but for now get your things. You too Elza. You are both coming to stay with me. Still frightened from what they just experienced they were glad to be going with Merlin.

Chapter 13
A Dreadful Disappearance

That evening they arrived at Merlin's house. They unpacked while Merlin made supper. "Now," Merlin said breaking the silence as they sat around the table. "I know you're both frightened but you must understand that when you're at school or with me I will make sure nothing like that happens again. Besides that man isn't the main problem of evil here. Someone stronger and much more powerful is the issue at hand here Merlin finished."

"Wait a minute," Walt looked confusingly at Merlin, "What your saying is that man isn't the problem we should be worrying about?" Walt asked.

"Who is this stronger person?" Elza interrupted "is he or she a wizard or witch?" she asked.

"Well what I'm saying is that the man who broke into Walt's house is another wizard's servant who was ordered to go to Walt's to try to steal the medallion. Now enough of this. Off to bed. You both need to have a good night's sleep so you're not tired on your first day back at the academy tomorrow." Merlin said as they all got up from the table.

They went to bed early so they wouldn't be tired for the busy day ahead. Walt had a dream one that he hadn't had before.

In the dream he saw himself as a man standing in the middle of a forest very smoggy and dark. It was night time as if had been in reality. The cold air numbing his cheeks. A young woman about his age was walking in the distance. Was that Elza? Walt's older self wondered. No it couldn't be. Then a dark shadowy figure ran at the woman, she let out a blood curdling scream and Walt woke with a start.

Walt felt himself jump out of his bed and run down the hall. He stopped at Elza's room and saw that the door had been blasted off its hinges. He looked across the still dark room to find her bed empty.

He felt a draft of cold air blow in from the open window. Merlin was lying on the floor unconscious his wand inches away from his lifeless body.

What had gone on while Walt was asleep and why hadn't he heard the noise? This was all a mystery. The only thing Walt did know was that Elza was missing and he didn't know what to do next.

Chapter 14
Back to the Academy

Walt felt the wind on his face as he flew through the air on Ickaris's back. He was on his way back to the academy. Merlin decided to meet him there in a few days due to Elza's disappearance

He wanted to find out who took her and why although he had an idea who could be behind it he wanted to be sure. Walt soon saw the castle in the distance and began to descend coming closer and closer to the ground. He told Ickaris to fly home to check on Merlin again Ickaris took to the skies.

Walt entered the school going straight to his room to put his things away. He was unpacking when he heard Tom his roommate come in.

"Hello, Walt," Tom said. "How was your vacation?" "Oh, err great. Yours?" Walt asked calmly.

"Oh, great I got some cool stuff I'll show you later. Hey I never saw Elza come in with you. Where is she anyway?" Tom asked. "You seem sad. What's wrong? Is everything okay?" He asked.

"Sit, I'll tell you but you can't tell anyone else, ok? Promise?" Walt asked.

"Uh, oh okay," Tom eyed Walt suspiciously. The grounds became dark, it seemed like everyone was in their rooms talking about their holiday break.

Soon it was supper time; Walt went down to the dining room with Tom. They found a table near the back where no one else was sitting to try to figure out what they could do to find Elza and her kidnapper.

"So now you know what I did over my break. Exciting, right?" Walt asked. Tom knew he was sad from the sound of his voice.

"I'm sorry about what happened because I know you care about Elza a lot."

"I don't want to talk about it anymore," Walt said. Supper ended, Walt went up to his room alone and found a note on his bed.

"If you ever want to see Elza again you won't come looking for me. If you try I will know. I do have people watching your every move. P.S. she's in good hands and I wouldn't tell your old oaf of a grandfather about this otherwise you may just make things worse." The Lord of Darkness: Mondomour

Walt didn't know who Mondomour was but he was sure this wouldn't be the last time he would hear his name. He folded up the note he would show Torn in the morning for now all he needed and wanted was sleep.

Chapter 15
Help from the Medallion

The next morning Walt went to breakfast alone. He planned to go looking for Elza in the afternoon during his lunch break and return to the castle that evening.

"Hey Walt," Tom said as he sat down by him. "Any luck finding Elza yet?" he asked.

"No," Walt replied wishing he could somehow change the subject. "I need to go. See you later," Walt quickly said choking down the last of his breakfast.

"Oh all right. See you later," Tom said. He walked as fast as he could out the maple wood front doors. He went to the back of the castle and called for Ickaris.

"Okay Ickaris we need to go see Merlin." With a great big bound Ickaris flew up beating his wings furiously. Soon the big castle was gone. Walt decided to start looking for Elza early for fear that something may happen to her the longer he waited. It was a cold morning like it had rained or the grounds had iced over the night before. Walt didn't like missing class but he knew if he had stayed at the castle Elza could be dead by late evening.

He landed outside Merlin's cottage rushing in. "Grandfather are you here?" Walt shouted into what seemed like an empty house. He heard shuffling and soon he saw his grandfather coming down the stairs.

"What are you doing here? You should be in class right now," Merlin said to him.

"I came to help you look for Elza. We need to find her," Walt said quickly.

"I've already told you I'm taking care of it," Merlin replied.

"I came to show you this," Walt said as he took the note out of his pocket and handed it to Merlin. He unfolded the piece of parchment reading it to himself.

"When did you get this?" Merlin asked.

"Last night," Walt replied, "why?"

"Come with me leave Ickaris here," Merlin said grabbing Walt and rushing out the door.

"Where are we going?" Walt asked suspiciously. "No time to explain. Come on hurry."

"But grandfather who is Mondomour and why does he want me to stay away from him?"

"Grab my arm! Hang on tight," Merlin said. "Soon they zipped through the air everything including time seemed to stop. Then Walt felt his feet touch solid ground again. It was still very dark and the smell of blood filled the air. "*Litrium,* " Merlin said and a light shot into the air from the tip of his wand.

"Where are we?" Walt asked. He could see that they were in a hall. He saw that the walls were a dark red color. They started moving down the hall soon coming to a door. "Stand back," Merlin said to Walt. He gave a swift flick of his wand and the door

blasted open Merlin ran in with Walt close behind. "Stop right there Mondomour!" Merlin yelled a wizard dressed in black robes turned very slowly to face them. His hands were raised in the air.

"Merlin, my old friend." said a raspy voice. "You found me. Oh and you brought your grandson. The one I have waited so long to meet. Walter, isn't it? Oh no, wait. Walt that is what you're called. Glad to meet you," said Mondomour.

"Shut up, Mondomour and show me where Elza is!" Walt screamed at him.

"Oh, she's right here. Son, bring the girl," Mondomour said into the darkness. "Oh, pardon me. I forgot to introduce my son Tom.

"Walt, he's told me so much about you," Mondomour said.

Sure enough Tom emerged from the darkness with Elza in his arms. Walt didn't know what to think as he saw one of his best friends carrying the girl he loved out to his father, the enemy.

Mondomour came into the light and Walt saw his face for the first time. He had long black hair and dark blue eyes. On his face he wore a crooked smile. "Thank you son," he said as he raised his wand. "Now I'm sorry, Tom, but when I sent you to the academy I was expecting a perfect trap for Merlin, Elza and of course Walt. But you betrayed me your own father. You made friends with the enemy forgetting about the job you were sent to do. So, I'm terribly sorry but I have no further tasks for you."

Walt could see Tom's face dripping with sweat. "Goodbye my son," Mondomour said loud enough for Walt and Merlin to hear.

"F-father no," Tom pleaded.

"Too late," Mondomour said. He aimed his wand right at Tom. *"Evica Lomorum!"* A jet of purple sparks flew at Tom hitting him right in the chest. Tom's lifeless body flew across the room, hit the wall and landed on the floor with a thud.

Then all of a sudden Mondomour disappeared.

Walt and Merlin ran to Tom's body in horror.

"Is there anything we can do?" Walt asked tears dripping off his face.

"No, it's too late," Merlin said. "Go to Elza and put the medallion around her neck," Merlin told Walt and he obeyed. When the medallion was around her neck a blue light shot out of it and her eyes opened.

"W-what, where am I? Walt is that you?" she asked him.

"Yes," he said his happiness returning. All he knew now was that even though he lost a close friend the girl he cared about most was back. He hugged her and helped her up. Then they took Tom's lifeless body back to the academy

Chapter 16
A Sad Goodbye

The next day, Tom's body was placed in a coffin that was protected by a magical enchantment which would prevent his body from going through any further harm. Walt, Merlin and Elza planned to have a proper funeral for Tom later that evening. As it started to get dark, they headed to an old unused church and buried Tom under a big willow.

Then Merlin started to speak. "We have gathered here today to say goodbye to a young yet great boy. Not just any boy a wizard who in the his last days of his life was good to everyone. Even though we couldn't prevent his death, he pleaded with his killer. All of us here know that if we could turn back time we would and we may have sacrificed our lives in order to save his. But it's too late now.

"If there is one thing we could do, we would like Tom's spirit to take these words of wisdom with him into the next life. Remember that nothing is impossible and we will never forget you, Tom. May you live on in our memories forever. May you rest in peace," he finished. Then Merlin, Walt and Elza covered Tom's casket with dirt.

After the hole was covered Merlin waved his wand and a white marble headstone was placed over the grave. The inscription read: *Here lies Tom. A young, yet powerful wizard who died too soon; but is remembered by all as a hero. May he rest in peace.*

Chapter 17
Mondomour and Merlin

The news of Tom's death reached the ears of hundreds of students at the academy. Most wondered how such a horrible thing could happen. Walt wrote to his parents and told them what had happened and that Elza, Merlin and himself were okay.

Both Elza and Walt wondered where Mondomour went after he killed his only son, and what did he plan to do next?

"I don't understand," said Elza to Walt when they were eating lunch a few days after returning to the academy. "Why would he kill Tom like that. I thought he was after the medallion?"

"Well," said Walt "he probably wanted to start something. Get the wizard army scared."

"So what you're saying is that he wants to go around killing people until a war breaks out?" Elza asked.

"Well, probably," Walt said.

Merlin was running down the corridor trying to catch Walt and Elza as they headed back to their rooms.

"Walt, Elza, I need you both to come to my office," he told them. They shuffled down the hall and soon came to the big oak doors and entered

Elza saw her guardians sitting in big wooden chairs around Merlin's desk. They ran to her and hugged her. There was a knock on the door. "Come in," Merlin said and a short stubby old man waddled into the room. "Oh hello, Professor Stumples," Merlin said.

"Merlin, I mean, headmaster. There's someone here to see you. He's standing outside.

"Oh, well okay. Thank you, Professor.

"Sorry to have to leave at such short notice I'll be right back if you don't mind waiting." Merlin left his office and strode out of the castle and across the grounds to see Mondomour waiting for him.

"What are you doing here! You have no right to be here!" "Draw your wand, old man! Show me what you can do!" Mondomour yelled.

"I don't want to fight you," Merlin said.

"What, are you scared? I won't kill you just yet."

"I don't need a wand," Merlin said. "I've beaten you before without a wand," Merlin replied getting angry. Merlin's hand flew skyward and Mondomour was pulled into the air.

"Put me down you idiot!" Mondomour yelled.

"Why should I? Are you scared?"

"I'll never be afraid of you," Mondomour said.

"You took my dream of working for King Arthur away from me and I'll never forgive you for that." Merlin waved his hand again and Mondomour flew higher than hit the ground with a bone breaking slam.

"You know that I won fair and square."

"You didn't win anything. He just liked you better."

"I have to get back to my office I have people waiting, so I'll make this fast. Why did you kidnap Elza and kill Tom?"

"Because firstly, my son is my business and he betrayed me by becoming friends with your grandson. So he deserved his fate. Then there's Elza. I knew that if I took her away from your protective walls I would find it easier to lure you to me and get the medallion. Not only that, but also I figured the best way to get my hands on the medallion was to cause a bit of trouble within your school thus frightening the king and queen causing them to take immediate action and thrust this country into a never ending war."

"Goodbye Merlin. See you in hell," said Mondomour as he waved his wand and disappeared.

Chapter 18
The War Begins

Walt was asleep in his room alone since Tom was now dead. He was suddenly awakened by a soft whisper outside his door.

"No, Edward, I have students to watch over. Their parents are counting on me."

"Merlin, he's in London. And who knows, if you don't come help now he'll kill the entire city then come for you."

"You mean he's killed people? How many?" Merlin asked aghast.

"At least ten. The wizard federal army is on their way to London now. They're probably surrounding the King and Queen's castle."

"But I have no one to keep things in order here and if I keep Walt here with the medallion then Mondomour will come to try to take it. Because that is what he wants. You know that."

"Well, then you must do something to keep it safe. Get it from Walt and put it somewhere where Mondomour can't get to it."

"I can't do that to Walt. He's had it for this long and nothing has happened."

"Well General Tumzil needs you there so do what you can before it's too late. Get back to me when you decide what to do."

"Is Mondomour getting any help?" asked Merlin.

"No, not yet. Anyway I have to get back before things get out of hand." Then with a wave of his wand and a loud crack Hucklesbey went back to London.

The next morning Walt awoke with beams of bright sunlight blinding him. Walt told Elza everything he had heard as he tried desperately to get some sleep the previous night. Elza's mouth flew open.

"So I was right about a war starting. Do you think your grandfather went to help?" she asked surprised at her own prediction.

"Well I'm assuming so because I haven't seen him all morning.

"Do you still have the medallion?" Elza asked.

"Yes," Walt replied.

"So what should we do?" Elza asked looking frightened. "Well I'm going to London after I'm done here to find Merlin."

Then home to get my parents if they aren't already there."

"Can I come?" Elza asked pleadingly. "I don't want Mondomour to hurt you again but I guess you probably should," he said. So they both left the academy on Ickaris' back hoping for the best.

They soon arrived in the center of London and met with their Walt's parents Elza's guardians and Merlin.

"We need to go to the central square to meet with the General and the other members of the army to see what they plan to do," said Merlin.

"Walt you stay here with us," said his parents. "Elza you too."

"I'll go speak with Edward while you all go to the square. See you later, Walt keep that medallion safe," Merlin said. "Dad, be careful," said Joe

"Don't worry I'll be fine," he said. They went their separate ways soon to meet up at the city square.

"Dad, why do you think Mondomour came here when he knew I had the medallion," Walt asked.

"He probably wanted to get everyone scared and make us know he's serious about this whole thing."

They reached the square to talk with the General.

"Well we need to wait and prepare the city. I've sent out troops to let us know when he comes until then all we do now is wait until nightfall," Tumzil finished.

Chapter 19
A Battle to Remember

Darkness came to London quickly. Walt, Elza, Walt's parents and the Henderson's waited with General Tumzil until the others came. Walt nor Elza had ever been in a war so they were both very nervous. More and more people crowded the streets to try and help before things got worse.

General Tumzil began to speak: "We all need to know we will stand together. No matter what happens we will stand together and fight until the end of this. Have your wands ready." All at once every single child and adult in the crowded streets held all of their wands high into the air.

Then Mondomour appeared with his army of evil wizards and witches behind him. Everyone in the city stood quietly as Mondomour began to speak. "Attention all people of London I came here for one thing and one thing only. I'll ask politely one last time. Walter I demand that you give me your medallion.

"Come here, boy. NOW!" he yelled.

"No," Walt said as he walked forward. "You'll never do anything to me that will make me give you my medallion. It will remain with me until I die!" he said angrily.

"So be it, die you shall," Mondomour yelled. "Attack!"

Then everyone evil or not cast spells everywhere. Things in all directions including people flew into the air; some were blasted back while others were killed.

Fires blazed, Walt and Mondomour were fighting in the middle of the city when a bluish white human - like figure came into view. "Hello Walt long time no see, how are things?"

"Tom is that you?" Walt asked the ghostly figure.

"Yes Walt it is. I came to help you win this war so that you can become what you've always dreamed of"

"What's that?" Walt asked.

"A hero, Walt a hero."

"How?"

"I'll show you use *Flameo Ascendo*, "Tom whispered. "Why? That's not to powerful," Walt replied.

"Do it! Believe me I'll protect you. I know his weakness after all. Sadly he is my father," Tom said laughing to himself.

"Okay here goes: *FLAMEO ASCENDO!*" Walt yelled and instead of a red flame a whitish blue stream of sparks shot out the end of Walt's wand and hit Mondomour. A white light filled the night sky then faded. Walt could see Mondomour lying on the ground however he knew that he couldn't possibly be dead.

Then Mondomour shot back up and pointed his wand threateningly at Walt.

"Goodbye grandson of Merlin," he said. "*Evica Lomorum!*" Walt was thrown backwards and hit the hard ground. He felt blood drip from his open skull. His eyes slowly closed. Elza, Merlin and Walt's parents cried out in horror.

Chapter 20
A Meeting with Death

Walt saw a bright light unlike the sun. He knew he wasn't in London anymore.

"Walt are you alright?" said a woman's voice.

"Who are you?" he asked her. She was dressed in a light red long dress and she had black hair.

"I am Ezra, Tom's mother. I was killed exactly how Tom was by his father. Now he's here with me, we can finally talk about so many things I've missed. Anyway you need to get back there and do something about my husband before he kills everyone" she said.

"What do you mean get back I'm dead," Walt replied.

"Yes you are but you forgot about one thing that medallion around your neck. It has the power to bring you back to life so you can never die. You're immortal. That's why my husband wants it now get back down there and be a hero" she said. "Goodbye, Walt. Nice meeting you."

Chapter 21
Back Again

Mondomour was about to take the medallion from Walt's neck when a sapphire blue light shot into the night sky. Walt's body rose high into the sky. His parents, Mondomour, Merlin, Elza and everyone else in the city watched in amazement.

Walt's eyes opened and his injury on the back of his head healed. It was as if he was being reborn. He landed safely on the ground.

"Impossible!" Mondomour said aghast.

"I forgot to mention," said Walt "this medallion makes me immortal. I'll never die as long as I have it with me."

Mondomour was immobilized by fear and astonishment. "Remember if you kill me today I will return," said Mondomour softly.

Everyone in the city was now on their feet watching in both fear and amazement. Walt slowly lifted his wand and pointed it at Mondomour.

"*Stonorium,* "Walt said.

Mondomour stood with his eyes wide as the spell penetrated him. Instead of knocking him backwards it froze him in place. Mondomour was now a statue of stone. All the dark wizards and witches disappeared now that their leader was stone.

Cheering and applause filled the city and at that moment Elza, her guardians, Merlin and Walt's parents encircled Walt in a joyful embrace. It was then that Walt knew Tom was right ... Walt was a hero.

Chapter 22
Walt the Wizard and the Sacred Medallion

Walt now knew why this medallion was sacred to his family. Not because so many people wanted it for world domination but because of its tremendous power. The city was renewed and everything that had been destroyed was restored, and Mondomour now a statue was not destroyed but taken to the museum of statues and placed in a vault that was heavily guarded.

The people who were killed were buried and honored for their heroism everything returned to normal. Walt and everyone else knew this war wasn't over. It was just beginning. Because as long as the medallion continued to exist there would always be the risk of evil hovering over the country. However for now Elza ,Walt and Merlin had to return to the Academy one last time.

Chapter 23
Celebrations

Before returning to the academy, everyone went to Walt's house to celebrate a great victory.

"I know this war isn't over." Joe said "but we decided to celebrate anyway The marvelous job our son and everyone else did.

I remember the day when I took Walt to a restaurant for lunch and he asked about our family. It was then that I gave him the medallion and told him he was a wizard and also about his grandfather. He didn't believe me at first but then he began training and was soon taken to the academy to learn more about the world of wizardry.

"I would like to take a moment to thank my dad for teaching him so much and making him stronger as well." They all applauded.

Then Merlin said, "When life gives you lemons you make lemonade." Then everyone including Merlin laughed into the night.

Chapter 24
Back to the Academy
For one last Time

Merlin took Walt and Elza back to the academy just in time to say goodbye and gather their things. Elza left after Merlin spoke to all the students. "I'll see you this summer maybe." Walt said as they said their goodbyes.

"Okay bye" Elza said.

They hugged each other one last time. Walt then went to his grandfather's office.

"Oh come in," Merlin said as Walt opened the big oak wood door. "Do you need help getting yourself home?"

"Oh no I'll fly on Ickaris he said." "I just wanted to thank you for everything you did for me this year."

"Oh well you're welcome and sorry I didn't explain the medallions power more to you. I should've said something.

"Oh no problem you just wanted me to figure it out on my own and I thank you for that too." He got up went over to Merlin and hugged him.

"Thank you for showing me what true magic is really like" he said.

"You're welcome grandson have a good summer." He said smiling at him. Then Walt left.

Chapter 25
Safe at Last

Walt was beginning to enjoy his summer away from school. He wrote to Elza everyday and occasionally went to see her.

He took her for a ride on Ickaris' back one sunny day and then they had a picnic together. He was really glad he met her because now that she was with him, he knew he wouldn't have to fight the dark magic of some other evil wizard they may have to fight in years to come alone.

They made a promise to each other never to leave each other no matter what happened.

Walt never told Elza however that he wasn't planning to go back to the academy next year. Its not that he didn't want to but because of all the memories he would have to face if he would go back. The memory of Elza being kidnapped and the death of one of his closest friends. He was glad that none of these things happened inside the walls of the academy but he still would remember those sad and painful memories.

He learned a lot outside the academy: how to love, how to feel pain, how to make lifelong friends, but most of all how to become a very smart and powerful wizard!

Chapter 1
The Meeting of Royalty

The city of London was busy with people on every street and every block. They were waiting for the King and Queen of England to decide what they would do about the problem at the Museum of Statues earlier that day.

"There's a problem here, Your Majesties. The city of London and even the whole world could be in danger if Mondomour and his army are not stopped," Merlin said.

"We know Merlin," the King replied. "But before we do anything to drastic, my wife and I would like our daughter to come home to the castle."

"Oh yes, of course. I'll get her as soon as I can," Merlin responded.

"You are dismissed, old friend," the King said kindly. Then Merlin casually walked out of the castle and disappeared. The King and Queen walked out to the castle balcony to address the people. They both had worried looks on their faces. The balcony doors opened and every man, woman and child looked up at the King and Queen awaiting their decision.

"People of London, we have decided to wait for our daughter's return to the castle before making any decisions. That is all." The King gestured for the gathering to disperse.

All the streets were clear within a matter of minutes.

"Walter, your grandfather is here. He would like to speak with you," Walt's mother yelled to him in his room.

An older more mature Walt came running down the stairs. "Hello, Grandfather," Walt said to Merlin.

"Hello, Walter. I need to take you to the center of London to speak to the King and Queen. We also need to pick up Elza on our way," said Merlin.

They were now outside walking down the street. "Wait! What is this about?"

"Why does Elza need to come with us?" asked Walt.

"Look at this." Merlin removed a newspaper clipping from his cloak pocket. Walt noticed it was dated a few months ago. Walt's eyes skimmed the clipping very quickly and his mouth dropped open at what he read.

Chapter 2
Elza Goes Home

"Why didn't you tell me you are the daughter of the King and Queen?" Walt asked Elza furiously.

"Walt, I thought you wouldn't like me anymore and maybe you would go after some other girl," Elza replied with tears in her eyes.

"Look, I'm sorry for getting angry and yelling like that. I just wish you would have told me who you are when we first met. I will always love you and only you, every day of my life," Walt said passionately.

They walked hand in hand through the royal garden and through the back entrance of the castle. Elza took Walt into the throne room to introduce him to her parents. Walt felt weak in the knees at the moment. Here he stood, not only in front of the rulers of his country, but also the parents of the girl he loved.

Elza spoke up. "Mum and Dad, this is my boyfriend Walt. He and I care deeply for one another and I hope you can get to know who he really is before deciding whether or not he is worthy enough to date me."

Walt bowed down in front of them to show his respect. "Very nice to finally meet you. I was quite surprised to learn Elza was royalty," Walt spoke. "We have known each other for a few years and I had no idea Elza was of royal blood. I am very much honored to know that you are her parents. She is a sweet, honest and purely perfect person in my eyes."

Walt had now been formally introduced to the King and Queen, or correctly known to him as Elza's Royal Parents.

"What's bothering you now?" Elza asked looking up at Walt a few minutes later.

"I'm just thinking of how it would have been if Tom were still alive. He probably would have been as shocked as I am to find out that you are part of the royal family," Walt said with sadness in his voice.

"Everything is changing so fast. People are dying. I have had to return to the castle," Elza said.

"I'll still come to see you every day. I promise," Walt replied.

"But now that I'm back home living in the castle it will be harder for us to spend time together. Every reporter in England will want to interview me," Elza said to Walt.

"Will your parents allow this?" Walt asked her.

"I don't know since I just returned home," Elza replied. "I heard mum and dad visiting last night in the great hall and they were talking about having a ball for me to celebrate my return home. I was hoping you would come."

"I will if my grandfather comes. My parents will allow me to come I'm sure," Walt replied. He then got up said goodbye to Elza, kissed her and left through the back gate of the castle.

Chapter 3
Mondomour's Plan

That evening on the darker side of England there stood a cliff that was wound like a snake and on the very top stood Mondomour's castle. He was in the top most towers of the castle plotting Merlin's downfall and a way to seize the medallion, and soon after all of England.

"So they thought they all could stop me," Mondomour said to himself. Not this time he laughed. I Mondomour will kill Merlin and his filthy family, then take all of England and turn it into the biggest evil empire this world has ever seen. I'll see to it that all evil wizards and witches join my army and I will then be King Mondomour wizard of darkness. I will lure them all to the docks, the whole city and then they will witness the end of all humanity.

"Since I broke out of that stone prison I have learned the art of shape shifting and with it the power to eliminate all humans from this continent leaving only me and my army. Things will be as they should have been in the days of King Arthur," he finished laughing evilly.

Chapter 4
The Ball

The next day Walt went to the castle early to ask the King and Queen a few things. He walked up to the gate and the guard smiled at him.

"Here to see Princess Elza I assume?" the guard asked with curiosity in his voice.

"No, not yet. I've actually come to see her parents I have something important to ask them," Walt said trying his best to keep his embarrassment from showing.

"If there's something that will not wait, then I suppose you should come right in," the guard said unlocking the gate. Then Walt hurriedly walked through almost tripping on his cloak as he entered the big oak doors.

"Hello there Walter how are you this very fine day?" said one of the butlers who happened to be strolling by the front doors as Walt entered.

"Oh, I'm just great I came to talk with Elza's parents."

"Ah... I see. Well then I'll leave you to your business see you later this evening than," the butler said quickly scurrying towards the kitchens.

Finally Walt was alone to gather his thoughts continuing to the throne room where he was hoping to find Elza's parents. At the throne room doors he clutched one of the big brass knobs and knocked.

He waited a moment then heard the king's voice from behind the doors.

"Come in." Walt pushed open the door with as much power as his muscles would give him. "Why are they so heavy?" he wondered, but soon pushed the thought from his mind. He looked ahead to see the King alone waving his wand two and fro hanging decorations for the evening festivities.

"Walter, what a surprise. If you're looking for Elza she's gone with her mother into the city to look for a new dress for this evening."The King lowered his wand and smiled at Walt.

"Um...actually sir I was hoping I could ask you something." Walt tried to keep his embarrassment from showing.

"Well I'm quite busy but I suppose I could take a minute to speak with you. What is it?"

Walt was searching for the right words to say and soon realized he was sweating terribly.

"Well, don't be afraid. Let it out," the King said breaking the uncomfortable silence.

Walt took a deep breath."Sir, I don't quite know how to say this so just hear me out before you say anything." Walt looked at his feet and realized he was shuffling them. "As you and your wife know I care deeply for your daughter. To be honest there isn't anything I wouldn't do for her. I realize you both just met me and you also may not like me all that much. However I truly love your daughter," Walt said now looking at the King face to face.

"I think I know where this is going. Come have a seat!" the King motioned for Walt to follow him. Sitting at his throne he made a gesture for Walt to sit next to him in Elza's throne.

"You seem nervous. Not to worry, boy. Elza's mother and I like you very much. We couldn't ask for a better companion for our daughter. "I know you have come here with hopes of getting my permission to marry Elza," the King paused. "I'm not saying `no' but at the same time I don't know whether to say `yes' either. Your love for each other is even stronger than mine for my dear wife at your age. I just want to know if you understand what marrying my daughter will mean," the King said.

"I know we're both very young but I can't envision myself with anyone other than your daughter. I'm also willing to assume any responsibility that I must in order to marry your daughter," Walt said his heart nearly ripping through his chest.

"My boy you never have failed to amuse me." the King smirked. "What I mean is do you think you could rule this country as it's next king? It is a very big responsibility you know and if you don't see yourself willing to take the necessary steps to becoming the king, I'm afraid I cannot give you permission to have my daughters hand in marriage. Don't worry about your age because to tell you the truth I was around your age when I married too."

"You were!" Walt said with surprise on his face and in his voice.

"Yes and I was about as nervous as you are too. Marriage is a big commitment it is one that once is promised should never be broken no matter what. I give you permission if you're willing to promise me one thing."

"Anything sir!" I swear to you I will do whatever you ask Walt said smiling nearly jumping to his feet to hug the King.

"Promise me you will become the heir to this throne and the castle. Also promise to never leave my Elza. Stay with her and make her happier than any other girl on this planet. If you fail to accept these responsibilities I will personally be sure to have you thrown out of this country along with all your family members and you will never be able to set foot on British soil again. Do you accept my terms?" the King asked.

"I do, your highness. I promise to give this country the best king it has ever had. More importantly I swear on my life to be the best husband to your daughter that I can be, I will give her the best life she could possibly ask for and no less." Walt said trying his best to stay calm.

"Then I, King Orville, am proud to give you permission to have my daughter's hand in marriage and I am proud to personally welcome you to our family. I am also prepared to have you as my new son-in-law," the King said shaking hands with Walt. "Welcome to' the family," he said again getting up and sweeping Walt into his arms for a hug.

Walt then got up, thanked the King red-faced and smiling and turned for the castle doors. Once again outside Walt called his dragon, Ickaris, and flew back to his house. Once on the ground in his yard Walt walked to the front door going inside to tell his parents the good news. It got late in the evening and soon Walt was ready to head back to the castle for the ball.

"Mum, Dad, I'm heading back to the castle now unless you want to go together," Walt called into his parents' room. His father came out closing the door behind him.

"Before you leave son I want to have a quick word," he said going to the couch and sitting. Walt joined him waiting for him to say what he wanted to say.

"What is it? I'm in a bit of a hurry so don't keep me too long," Walt said leaning back resting his head on the cushion.

"What I want to say is something I wish I would've mentioned before but haven't had the time, your mum is in our room trying her best to remain calm she is still in shock that you asked King Orville to marry Elza. To tell you the truth I don't think she is quite ready for this and I don't know if I am either," Walt's dad replied calmly.

"Dad the King and I talked about everything, I realize we're both very young. I promised him I would do everything I could to be the best husband to Elza and very best king to this country. He has given me permission to marry her and I believe this is what Elza wants too. You and mum just have to trust me on this and believe that I'm true to my word," Walt said getting annoyed with all this trust talk.

"Walt I'm not saying you can't do this but what I mean is once you marry things are going to change, Mondomour will find out, your mother and I are just afraid of what could happen. We want the both of you to have a wonderful life together. We have no doubt that you both are very ready for this regardless of your age. You two it seems were made for each other and haven't left each other since the day you both met. All we are asking as your parents is that you do everything to keep any harm from coming to the family. We would hate for something bad to happen to either of you. Becoming king will only add to your responsibility, you won't just have a family to take care of but also this entire country. Both Elza's and your decisions will not only impact what happens within our families but they will also greatly impact our country's future. We are proud of who you have become and we know that your destined to be an even greater wizard in the coming years. We are happy for you and hope everything goes well tonight no matter what Elza's decision is," Walt's dad said catching his breath.

"Dad as much as I appreciate your blessing I really should be going so I can gather my thoughts and possibly be able to think of what I would like to say to my future wife, that is if she agrees to marry me," Walt said getting up and moving towards the door.

"Wait Walt I would like you to give Elza this ring when you ask her to marry you it was my mother's she gave it to me just before she died she told me that once you marry that I was to give it to you to give to your wife" Walt's dad replied pulling a ring from his pocket that Walt noticed had a very big diamond in the center.

"Dad I don't know what to say," Walt said taking the ring from his father and examining it.

"Don't worry son I'm almost sure she'll say yes at least that's what my heart feels but if for some reason I'm wrong always remember you will be welcome here," Walt's dad said hugging him. Remember to enjoy yourself tonight, don't get to upset if things don't go the way you hope.

"I think things will go just fine, thank you again dad I'll see you later," Walt said smiling at his dad as he went out the door. "Okay Ickaris lets head back to the castle for the ball," Walt said to Ickaris climbing on his back. Ickaris then spread his big wings lunging into the air flapping them a few times to stay airborne. Soon they arrived at the drawbridge once again the guard opened the gate for Walt to enter. Once inside Walt went directly to the throne room pushing the doors open. He saw Elza sitting in her new throne talking with her parents, they all looked up as the doors slid closed behind Walt as he entered. Elza was wearing a big sparkly white dress with red lace at the corners. She ran up to him when she saw him enter the room.

"Thank you for coming," Elza said hugging him. Then she showed him the ball room and the royal dining room where the activities would take place. Soon guests started to arrive there were a few dukes and duchesses' but most who came were members of Elza's family. Walt noticed that Elza's family wasn't very large, he found this quite unusual because of her nobility but soon ignored the thought. He went to speak with his parents and grandfather when they arrived. While Elza was bombarded by her family members. Soon the King and Queen announced it was time for supper. Everyone began to make their way into the royal dining room. Once everyone was seated the cooks and other attendants started bringing out the many dishes they had prepared, everyone around the long table filled their plates. The King stood and everyone stopped what they were doing patiently waiting for him to speak.

"Attention I would like to purpose a toast to my beautiful daughter Elza and her very wonderful boyfriend Walter. I am honored that he saved our daughter's life three years ago, I also want to thank you for bringing her home to us" he finished. Everyone applauded and they all went back to eating and visiting.

"You're welcome" he whispered to Elza's parents and continued eating. When everyone was finished eating they gathered in the ballroom and soon music echoed off every wall and everyone began to dance.

"Walt dance with me," Elza said coming over to Walt where he was sitting at a table alone.

"Okay," he replied standing and taking her hand. They moved out to the middle of the dance floor and Walt spun Elza around and around. "Elza I need to ask you something," Walt whispered in Elza's ear as the song came to an end minutes later.

Yes what is it?" she asked now looking him in the eyes still whispering.

"I know we've only known each other for three years but I know if I don't do this now it may be too late later. I may not even get another chance," he paused a moment then continued. "So" he said turning red in the face and bending down on one knee "Will you marry me?" he said as he held out the big diamond ring his father had given him earlier. Elza's mouth fell open and she started to cry.

"Yes Walter I would be honored to marry you," she replied taking the rig from him. Walt got up hugging and kissing her. Both Walt and Elza continued to enjoy the ball dancing all night with smiles on their faces. They both knew that this was now one of the best days of their lives.

Chapter 5
The Battle on the Docks

W alt visited Elza every day after the ball talking to her about wedding plans. The King and Queen seemed very excited about the wedding almost as much as Elza and Walt.

Meanwhile Mondomour also was busy getting things ready to carry out his plan for the city which he planned to execute later that evening. "Showtime" said Mondomour once he had his plan in order. Then he disappeared. Merlin was in the city with Walt's father sitting in a coffee shop discussing the headline in the morning paper.

"Look" said Walt's father. "The news of Walt and Elza's engagement has reached the public eye should we be concerned?" He asked.

"Nonsense. News such as this travels fast especially in this big city," Merlin replied. Wait speaking of that I remember having some sort of dream or vision that involved Mondomour," Merlin said looking about frantically.

"Well what do you mean when did it happen? What did it show you?" Walt's father asked nervously.

"Well I believe he wanted to lure the people in London somewhere in order to end the lives of those who wouldn't agree to name him king and swear allegiance to his dark ways. He also wants to kill the King and Queen then he plans to capture Liza again," Merlin finished rising from the table.

"Well when does he expect to do all of this without getting caught?" Walt's dad said also standing preparing to leave.

"That I don't know but we must hurry we have to warn Elza and her parents!" Merlin said moving quickly. "In order for everyone to stay safe we need to act fast" Merlin said now outside running towards the castle with Joe at his heels.

Suddenly as they left the city square heading for the castle they heard a woman scream somewhere in the city.

"He's back and he is heading for the shipyard! Inform the King and Queen!" she yelled to a guard. Merlin raised his wand to his throat.

"No Stop! That is what he wants you to do!." His voice echoed throughout the square. "Let's go" he said to Walt's father who had his wand drawn.

"All right" he replied to Merlin. They both aimed their wands at the ground and said *"Flyo Arasio"* and soared into the air. They landed on the shipyard docks ready for Mondomour. Than he was there as quick as the wind.

"Hello, oh look father and son together come to try and stop me have you?" Mondomour laughed.

"*Evica Lomorum*" Merlin said. "Mondomour dodged the curse.

"So 'hats the way you want to duel is it? he said. He aimed his wand at Walt's dad. "*Evica Lomorum*" the curse hit him square on the chest and he flew into the water. Walt's father's lifeless body was floating on the water.

Chapter 6
An Unexpected Turn

Merlin disappeared to Walt's house quickly to inform Walt and his mother about what had just happened down by the water's edge.

"How could it have happened like that?" "Did you find his body?" cried Jane.

"I have informed the Wizard League" Merlin informed her. "What's wrong?" Walt said as he ran into the dining room. "Your father is.. your father is dead because of Mondomour" his mother gasped and began to cry uncontrollably.

"Gone! "What do you mean gone?" Walt cried.

"No!" Merlin said. "Walt he is dead, and we don't know where his body is it flew into the water" Merlin tried to explain.

"I can't believe this!" "That ungrateful, disgrace to humanity," Walt yelled out. "I need to go," Walt said with tears in his eyes. "I may be home late!" he said as he slammed the door behind himself.

Chapter 7
Revisiting Toms Grave

Walt decided he would go to Toms' grave for a while to help forget about what he had just learned. He called Ickaris. Then flew to the place where Tom was buried. As soon as he landed he sat beside the grave letting his feeling go through hint

"Walt what is wrong?" said a voice.

Walt froze. "Tom is that you?" he called out into the still evening. Then everything was silent again. He knew that voice he was sure he did. "Tom!" Walt called out again. The air got colder and Walt saw a white figure float done beside him. "Tom is that you?" Walt asked.

"Yes it is Walt" and it's nice to see you again" replied Tom.

It was as though he were still alive. "Is everything okay Walt?" "What happened?"

"Well my mother has just told me that my father has been murdered by your father" Walt cried. "I don't know what to do or what to believe."

"What how he can't be dead!" Tom said aghast.

"Well surprise he is" and I just need some time alone right now," Walt replied with anger in his voice. "Oh one more thing I found out Elza is the King and Queen's daughter and I've asked her to marry me just thought you should know."

Then he told Ickaris to fly home. He took out his wand and yelled, "*Disappearo*" and disappeared. Tom tried to tell him to come back but it was too late, Walt was already gone. It was at that moment Tom knew things were about to take a turn for the worst.

Chapter 8
The Army of Evil

"I can't stand this anymore!" Walt said to Merlin while walking to Merlin's house.

"Calm down, Walt. I know that your father isn't dead. At least not yet I have found one of my old spell books and in it I found the spell of recovery," he said happily.

"Yeah ... so what does the spell do?" Walt asked him.

"It allows a person that has been injured or possibly killed by a very powerful curse to reawaken and live as they once did," Merlin responded.

"Wait what do you mean by reawaken and what about the persons memories?" Walt replied. "Won't those be gone?" Walt asked becoming worried and confused.

"Well I've only tried the spell once long ago on a mouse, so I know it works for animals," Merlin said with a bit of worry in his voice. "I'm not entirely positive it will work on a human let alone save all of their memories," Merlin said adding to the worry in

Walt's gut. They arrived at the door of Merlin's house and they went inside.

"Just a minute I need to go get the book," Merlin said heading up the stairs. He came back down a few minutes later with a very large, very old looking spell book clutched in both hands.

"Here it is," Merlin said gazing intently at the book. "Grandfather wouldn't we need dad's body in order to do this?" Walt asked wondering what his grandfather had in mind. "Why yes Walt not to worry that has been taken care of'

Merlin replied grinning.

"But I thought you said he sunk in the harbor," Walt asked with a confused look on his face.

"He did my boy however later that night I went searching for him and found him on the very bottom," Merlin said happily.

"But how?" Walt asked.

"I swam to the bottom of course," he said laughing to himself. Meanwhile back on the dark side of England Mondomour was building his army, to take over England and capture Elza and dethrone the King and Queen.

"I still don't understand why I hadn't found all of you great creatures and dark wizards sooner?" Mondomour said to a crowd full of trolls, mutant lizard like beings, witches, wizards and many other horrific creatures who crammed into the throne room of his castle. "Now my plan is to take over England, take the medallion and soon the whole world. This can come true with all of you behind me," Mondomour said to the creatures while standing in front of his throne. "Then with your aid I can kill anyone who stands in my way," Mondomour said before his new followers. "Soon I will be able to build my evil empire and then become Mondomour the lord and king of all darkness and of the world!" Mondomour said evilly. "Soon my minions we will strike and make the world ours" he finished. Then the castle erupted in furious laugher and cheering.

Chapter 9
Walt's Dad Returns

Merlin and Walt were walking to a concealed area in the forest just beyond the castle where no one could see what they were doing when they saw a very old woman appear out of nowhere.

"Who is that?" Walt asked his grandfather. Merlin was still he quietly raised his wand.

"*Invisious Disappearo*" he whispered then he and Walt disappeared. Now both invisible they slowly and quietly crept deeper into the forest. Once they were far enough away not to be seen or heard Merlin lifted the spell .

"Who is that woman?" Walt asked again. Merlin was still very silent. "You know who that is don't you?" Walt said suspiciously waiting for a response from his grandfather.

"Yes," Merlin finally said. "But she's no one who you would want to cross paths with," he said raising his eyebrows.

"Who is she then?" Walt asked again.

"I'll tell you later now quickly before she finds us."
"We must reawaken your father," Merlin said moving quickly over to another well hidden area where Merlin pulled out Walt's father. Walt knew that Merlin hated telling him about strange people but he wanted to know what was so secretive about his grandfathers past. Why did he keep every secret he had from everyone else? Merlin now was performing the spell of recovery on Walt's father. Walt stood a few feet away watching intently. "I call upon you angels of heaven bring back to this world what was once lost to the doors of death, give this lifeless body back its breath make this mortal live again. Only when you need him most will he then be taken. Heaven, hell or limbo he will then stay, just let him live out the rest of his days." Merlin finished closing the big book. Then in the blink of an eye Walt's father rose into the air and opened his eyes. A white light went straight through him as he was slowly brought back down to the ground very much alive. Walt ran to him and hugged him.

"I thought you'd never come back," he cried as he hugged his father as if he had just come home from war.

"I'm grateful to be back too son," Walt's father replied. Then they walked out of the forest into the morning sun ready to go home as a family again.

Chapter 10
The War Thickens

S oon news of Mondomour's army and his plans to take over London reached the ears of all people throughout the city of London including the King and Queen's.

"We need to find Mondomour and his army before he decides to kill more people or worse take over the city Elza told her parents becoming worried.

"We know Elza dear, your mother and I are trying our best to keep everyone safe," the King replied trying to calm his daughter down.

"You may think you have everything under control however my future husband is the one Mondomour wants!" "Do you know why?" Elza said looking at both of her parents. "He has the medallion that Mondomour wants!" Elza said becoming even more upset by the minute.

"We know about the medallion and we realize your upset but we're doing all we can, her father said trying his best to keep his temper at bay.

"All we can do now is ask the Prime Minister for help," the Queen retorted.

"Oh so now you think by getting the Prime Minister a man with no magic blood what so ever to help we might be able to win this war?" "Well don't you know who you're dealing with?" she replied to her parents angrily!

"Elza we understand that all of this is troubling for you and everyone else, even if your mother and I go find Mondomour and fight him with our magic it may not be strong enough and we could lose against him. The castle and the country would be easier to take over!" the King said throwing his hands in the air.

"Oh I get it you think Walt and I won't be able to handle the responsibilities as King and Queen?" "Well I hate to prove you wrong mum and dad but I am a more powerful witch now. With Walt and Merlin by my side we will make it through this alive and together," Elza said looking up at the ceiling in frustration. "I've faced Mondomour before, I know his power!" she said yelling now.

"That's exactly it you weren't alone last time and Mondomour isn't anymore either. So you can bet he'll be stronger and ready with a plan," the Queen said.

"I can't take this anymore I need to go," said Elza turning her back on her parents running from the throne room. Tears streaming down her face.

Chapter 11
Under Attack

It was a bright sunny morning in London everyone seemed to be in a good mood but what the city's inhabitants didn't know was that everything was about to change forever. A man in a very dark black hooded cloak walked down the street. The man was a wizard few people that were in the center of the city could tell from the way he was dressed. The man stopped on a street corner and began to shuffle in his pockets. He pulled out what some passersby knew was a wand the man slowly raised it up into the air.

He then yelled: "Darkness of evil, darkness of night fill this city with fright, make the sky as dark as night!" Then suddenly from the man's wand tip a jet of dark black smoke and fog filled the air. The wind came up and started to howl and a man standing outside of a coffee shop quickly looked up and saw that the hooded man was none other than Mondomour.

"Mondomour is back everyone run for your lives!" the man screamed at the top of his lungs. Then out of nowhere Mondomour's army flooded the city. Soon sparks from wands, shrieks of death and pain filled the air.

"Yes my time to become king of England and soon the whole world has come," he laughed in his evil raspy laugh. "I only need to kill the King and Queen. Then I will get the medallion and kill Walt along with his family. Then I will be lord and supreme king of all darkness" Mondomour said even louder. Merlin began hearing screams as he came into the city with Walt and his parents.

"This is terrible we weren't ready, he's begun his takeover. I will go to the castle to get the King, Queen and Elza to help fend Mondomour off. For now all of you get in there and try to stop this before something bad happens. Walt hold off Mondomour, you two protect him. I don't want another death. I'll be back very soon stay together." Merlin said just before disappearing. They all ran for the center of the city dodging spells of all sorts. Walt took out his wand quickly and aimed for Mondomour.

"*Flameo Ascendo!*" he yelled. Flames shot from the end of it. Mondomour quickly looked up and swept the flames away with his hand. He saw Walt with his parents standing inches away from him. Their wands out ready for anything.

"Well, well, well look who it is Walter and his parents" he paused then continued again. "I thought I killed you?" he said looking at Walt's father shocked to see him alive. Merlin than appeared right next to his son along with Elza, the King and Queen.

"Oh well now this is literally one of the greatest days of my life," Mondomour said laughing loudly. "All the people I've been wanting and waiting to kill all show up in the same place just to welcome their new king," he said to all of them smiling evilly.

"I don't think you're going to get that chance," Elza said pointing her wand threateningly at Mondomour.

"Take your best shot" Walt said. "Is this what you want?" Walt said showing Mondomour the sapphire blue medallion he had hidden behind his shirt hanging from his neck.

Mondomour froze "Yes your right the last time you used it to turn me to stone and then fled. However I escaped and regained the power to shape shift," he said smirking at them. "Now I will show you what I mean," he said as he flew into the dark sky. He looked as if he were a marionette with strings attached to his every limb. Then right before everyone's eyes he turned into a fierce dragon. He lunged at Walt and his family only missing them by inches. Then out of anger he took a deep breath and black flames shot out of his mouth.

"Okay so you think that's all I have," Mondomour said in a very deep voice. Then once again he transformed into a big troll with a spiked club. Coming to the ground with an earth splitting bang. He was about to swing his club when Walt interrupted him.

"Wait, stop!" he yelled quickly. "You want this don't you?" he asked. Mondomour shook his tiny troll head. "Then in order to get it you'll have to fight me first," Walt said looking up at Mondomour. Soon

Mondomour started returning to normal size his club disappearing Now back to normal Mondomour stood thinking about the offer placed before him and his chance to finally make the medallion his.

"All right than," he replied drawing his wand. "On one condition you may not get any help from others around you," Mondomour said smiling to himself Thinking that he had out smarted Walt.

"All right than agreed," he said. "But I also have a request you cannot kill any more people and no help from your army either," Walt said smirking at Mondomour. Mondomour hesitated a moment.

"Agreed a battle to the death," he quickly said laughing. Elza and the others gave a shriek of horror at the agreement between Walt and Mondomour.

"Give me everything you've got!" shouted Walt drawing his wand.

Chapter 12
A Battle to Remember

Everyone in the city did not want this to happen, however they knew it was the only way to save England let alone the world. This was what needed to happen in order to stop a power so evil and heartless from spreading. So everyone except Walt and Mondomour could only hope for the worst or best depending on whose side you were on, bystanders could only watch awestruck waiting to see who would be victorious.

"*Evica Lomorum!*" Mondomour screamed.

"*Oblivia!*" Walt quickly said. Soon the whole city was brightened by the two powerful curses. These curses were created by the wands of two of the most powerful wizards the world had ever known.

"You know," Mondomour yelled over the noise of the curses. "I have been waiting for this moment almost my entire life. You can quit now if you want. It would make things better for the both of us," he said laughing but keeping a firm grip on his wand.

"Not a chance, I would never let you win and watch my castle along with the people I love be tortured or worse destroyed by you or your army" Walt screamed back at him.

"Oh what a noble soon to be king," he laughed. Then suddenly the medallion around Walt's neck started to glow bright blue, at that same moment Walt's curse hit Mondomour right in the heart. He flew up into the air and evaporated into a puff of red and black smoke. Everyone closed their eyes and when they opened them Mondomour and his evil army were gone.

Light returned to the city in a rush and the people's hearts were once again filled with peace.

Chapter 13
A New King

Today was the day almost everyone in the city had been waiting for it was the day a new King and Queen would be crowned. Walt was pacing the castles hallways he felt strange walking in the castle. He remembered when he would walk outside the castle as a boy and be so envious of the King and Queen. That was before he met Elza of course. Now he felt even more awkward because the feelings inside of him.

"Stop" Elza told him. "You're making me nervous," she said smiling at him trying to hide her true feelings.

"Oh sorry I guess you haven't noticed that you're not the only one," Walt said finally stopping and smiling at her. Elza's mother and father came in along with Walt's parents. Elza's parents told her that she needed to go get ready for the crowning leaving Walt alone in the big throne room. Walt stood gazing at every wall thinking about how things would be once he and Elza ruled.

"Wonderful isn't it?" said a familiar voice. Walt turned quickly to see Merlin standing behind him.

"I'm not ready for this," Walt said to his grandfather slowly taking a breath.

"I know that you're nervous however you must realize that once you marry Elza you have no choice. You must accept the crown," Merlin said looking at his grandson and smiling.

"I know but what if nobody likes the way I lead them?" he asked nervously.

"You won't be alone and everyone has been waiting for this day," Merlin said putting a hand on Walt's shoulder to reassure him.

"Well I guess but I thought Elza's parents ruled until they died?" Walt asked suspiciously.

"Well they would however they decided to let you and Elza become King and Queen now so that they could see their daughter get the crown before they die," Merlin replied.

"Oh I didn't know that was allowed," Walt said surprised. Then trumpets sounded and cheering could be heard outside the castle walls. Walt took one look at his clothes than took out his wand. He gave it a wave turning his old clothes into the finest indigo blue garments that Merlin had ever seen. They also came with a velvet black cloak that was trimmed with white around the edges.

"How do I look?" he asked Merlin.

"You look like you were born to be a king," Merlin said smiling and nodding at his newly prepared clothing. "Are you ready?" Merlin asked him.

Walt took a deep breath and said confidently. "As ready as I will ever be," Than he and Merlin walked to the balcony curtains waiting for Elza, her parents and Walt's parents to return from the inner rooms of the castle. They smiled at each other happily.

Chapter 14
The Passing of the Crown

Elza came with the others and took her place beside Walt and Merlin waiting patiently. The curtains opened and Elza's parents stepped out onto the balcony. Thousands of people who flooded the streets below cheered. The King made a signal then the crowd went quiet.

"Thank you all for coming here on this wonderful day. My wife, I hope you will honor and be loyal to your new King and Queen" said the King loudly so that everyone could hear him. He then issued for Walt and Elza to come out onto the balcony.

"It gives me great pleasure to introduce to you our daughter Princess Elza and the grandson of Merlin her fiancé Walter. The crowd cheered and Elza and Walt waved then moved aside and took seats on two big velvet red and gold thrones. Then the King took off his crown and told Walt to kneel before him. The crowd went quiet and Merlin and Walt's parents smiled proudly. Walt's mother began to cry still smiling. The King drew his sword.

"I King Orville the first dub thee King Walter and swear you into the royal family. From this day forward let you lead England as its next King" Orville finished touching his swords blade to both of Walt's shoulders. He sheathed his sword and placed his golden crown on Walt's head. Walt stood up sitting back down in his new throne. The Queen told Elza to kneel before her and she then removed her crown. "I queen Madelyn the first dub thee Princess Elza Queen of all England," Madelyn said placing her crown on Elza's head. Elza stood and sat beside Walt in her throne. Then Orville and Madelyn said together,

"It is our great pleasure to introduce before this great city of London and all of England, your new King and Queen Walter and Elza." They both stood and walked forward to once again face the crowd. Cheering and trumpeting greeted the new King and Queen. Both Walt and Elza looked out at their followers waving and smiling to everyone very happy.

Chapter 15
Excalibur

Now that Walt and Elza were King and Queen all Walt's belongings were moved into the castle including Ickaris. Walt and Elza were walking peacefully one day in the royal gardens when hundreds of photographers and reporters who flocked outside the gates on a regular basis came running towards them. Reporters reached their arms in and photographers began snapping pictures. Everything was happening all so quickly. People started yelling for both Walt and Elza's attention and others who were outside the gate were being trampled by the large mobs of people just so someone could get a look at the two new leaders.

"Over here, Your Majesties!" a reporter yelled finally getting their attention. "What are your plans for the country now that you're both in command?" the reporter asked waiting for a reply.

"We don't know yet, we need to sit down and speak with parliament to see what they recommend and then we will make our decision based on what they believe is the best way to approach this," Walt said.

"Do you two have any plans for children after you're married?" asked another reporter who squeezed himself up to the gate.

"No comment," Elza and Walt said together.

"Guard! Can we get some privacy please?" Walt said after minutes of being bombarded with questions and blinded by camera flashes. A guard outside the gates then rushed over to rid them of the disturbance.

"Yes, Your Majesty." he said bowing to Walt and shooing everyone away.

Once they were alone Walt walked with Elza to the stone fountain in the center of the garden and sat down on an edge. "So, did your parents have to get through reporters and paparazzi like that too?" Walt asked looking at her.

"Well, when I was little it was like that before I left the castle for awhile. I can assume it was very much like that before I was here," Elza said smiling at him.

"I hope we don't have to deal with photographers or reporters every time we go outside the castle" Walt said putting his head in his hands. Elza could tell he was already getting annoyed, with the lack of privacy when in public.

"What did you expect? You and I are the king and queen now and the entire country needs us both to lead them," Elza said putting a hand on his shoulder.

"Well isn't that what the Prime Minister should be doing too?"

"Yes but he is not the only one involved in the city's political affairs" Elza said as Walt rose from the fountain. "I don't want to make this into an argument, so can we do something else rather than argue?" Elza said getting up and walking back toward the castle.

"If you want we could fly somewhere with Ickaris," he said pausing a moment to think. "We're not normal people anymore what am I thinking we can't just go off and do as we please," he said realizing his mistake.

"Yeah well that's easy for you to say I've never been normal" Elza said. "You only thought I was when you first met me," she said to him laughing.

"Okay I have an idea lets go see my grandfather, then after I will take my bride to be somewhere where we can be alone together like normal people for a few days," Walt said grabbing Elza's arm and drawing his wand with his free hand.

"*Disappearo*" Walt said and they vanished with a crack. They arrived outside of Merlin's house and knocked on the door.

"Oh hello come in!" he said opening the door surprised to see them and they walked inside.

"I'm glad you came I have something for you Walt," he said. "It's right on the table an old friend left it for you." "Who?" Walt asked.

"Just open it," Merlin replied. Walt came to his grandfather's small table and saw a long wooden box labeled with ancient writing. He began to open it carefully. He looked into the box and took out a sheath it was very heavy and old looking. Walt wobbled almost dropping the very old sword.

"It's a sword!" Walt replied very surprised. He withdrew it and stroked the shiny silver blade, beautifully crafted with ancient designs carved into the blade and handle.

"It was king Arthurs," Merlin said smiling at his grandson.

"What!" Walt said re-sheathing the sword and putting it away. "Are you telling me this sword is the one from the stone in the legends?" he asked his eyes nearly popping out of his head. "The same sword so many battles were won with,"

"Yes," Merlin said happily. "Arthur told me before you were born that he wanted you to have it once you became king." So the sword now belongs to you Walt.

"Wait so if this sword belonged to King Arthur and he told you to give it to me once I became king how did he know I would be alive or become the king?" Walt asked giving his grandfather a confused look.

"Your father became a knight for Arthur shortly before Arthur died, that is how your mother met your father." Merlin said trying his best to remember what happened so long ago.

"What? They have never told me this story before" Walt said shocked at what he had just heard. "What about my mum how is she involved in this?" he asked.

"Well she was one of Arthur's royal nurses who helped aid him while he was sick or injured" Merlin said trying to explain the story exactly how he remembered. Elza stood taking in the conversation silently.

She was also very proud of Walt. "Well thank you for giving me this and letting me know a lot about how this all came to be" Walt said smiling at his grandfather turning towards the door. They both said good bye to Merlin shutting the door behind them, heading back to the castle. Walt now carrying Arthur's sword Excalibur with them.

Chapter 16
Torn Apart

"We're leaving for a place where no one will find us," Walt said to Elza once they arrived back at the castle.

"What do you mean leaving?" Elza said heading outside again. "The country needs us. What if Mondomour attacks the city again while we're gone? Then what?" Elza said becoming angry.

"Mondomour is dead. You saw me kill him. You can't possibly think after all that fighting he would still be around," Walt said trying to remain calm while also trying to keep Elza from becoming more upset.

"You know as well as I do he is still alive and if we don't stay here he'll kill everyone!" Elza said insistently.

"All right then. If you want to stay here and constantly be swarmed by reporters and photographers, be my guest I'm leaving for a while so I can think!" Walt said holding back his anger.

"You don't even care that we are dealing with a killer and that our country, the place we now rule, is on the brink of war. You just want to go away and pretend everything is okay!" Elza said raising her voice. "You just asked me to marry you for the castle and the money, didn't you? You wanted power and used me to get it!" Elza yelled completely losing control. Tears ran down her face.

"You know that's not true! You're upset and I understand that. I told you why I wanted to marry you. I love you!" Walt said losing his patience.

"Besides we're not even married yet," he said sadly.

"You're right and that's why I need to do this before it's too late!" Elza said sobbing. She took a breath, "The wedding is off!" she screamed at him taking off the ring and throwing it at him. "Go away from the world and be afraid of everything and everyone, you filthy commoner!" she said turning and running from him.

Walt bent down and picked up the ring. He walked away and sat under an old oak in the royal gardens. He began to cry. He didn't want this to happen. Then he got up and ran quickly after Elza who was by now almost near the city.

"Wait! Elza please, we need to talk about this," Walt pleaded as he caught up with her.

"I don't want to anymore. You don't care. You said so yourself," she cried keeping her eyes on the ground. Walt grabbed her just as she was about to turn away from him He pulled her so close to him their faces were almost touching.

"Let go!" Elza demanded through clenched teeth as she tried to wriggle away from him.

"Stop please! You know I don't want to do this and I know you don't either," he said hugging her and holding out his hand.

Elza saw the ring and pushed away from him. "No Walt. I'm not ready yet," she said sniffling. I'm sorry." She looked up into his eyes. Then she took his hand and kissed it. After a moment she released his hand walking back towards the castle.

It was then that Walt called for Ickaris.

"Let's go. Ickaris. We need to get away for awhile. I need to think about some things," he told his dragon. Walt then took Ickaris into the air. He decided to go to someplace he liked to visit. "Across the channel to France," he commanded. He planned to stay there for a few days to clear his head and be away from everything else.

Chapter 17
Mondomour's Past

Walt and Ickaris arrived in Paris and made arrangements for a place to stay. Then Walt went out to stroll the streets. He had to disguise himself so no one would recognize him as the king of England. Otherwise he knew he would never have any time to think or be alone. While walking he saw Edward Hucklesbey his grandfather's friend.

"Oh hello, Your Majesty," Hucklesbey said after realizing it was Walt in a disguise. "Where is Elza?" Hucklesbey asked looking around for her.

"Well," Walt said as they walked down the street, "we had a little fight and she got quite upset with me." He took a long breath. "She took off her ring and threw it at me. Then she said the wedding was off." Walt looked ashamed of himself.

"My! How awful. Did you tell your grandfather or your parents about it?" Hucklesbey asked.

"No. I came straight here. I got a place to stay a few blocks down. I'll leave when I get everything straight and have had some time to think," Walt said starting to feel relieved to be away from England.

"I'm here on business so come to me if you need help," Hucklesbey said patting Walt on the back. He was about to walk away when Walt called after him.

"Edward, do you know anything about Mondomour's past?"

Hucklesbey turned back to Walt. "What do you want to know?"

"Different events, things about his past, what he was like as a child," Walt said trying to keep his voice low. "Tell me anything you know that may help me find him," Walt said.

"Why on earth would you want to find him?" Hucklesbey replied looking confused and shocked at the same time. "I thought you killed him?" Hucklesbey added.

"I want to be sure. Before I left Elza told me she believes he is probably still alive," Walt said. "She may be right. I thought if I knew about his past it might help me find out why he wanted this medallion so bad. It would also help to know his weaknesses," Walt said smiling.

"Let's go eat and then we can sit and talk about this together," Hucklesbey said. They found a pizzeria down the road. They entered the restaurant and the smell of freshly baked pizza filled the air.

"*Velcome to Parentello's Pizzeria. Right zis way,*" the host said taking them to a booth in the back of the tiny restaurant. "Le server will be ere momentarily," said the host giving them each a napkin and silverware.

Once they were alone Edward laughed at how the host talked in a funny way.

"I have to admit though as funny as I thought that was he did seem to speak pretty good English considering this is France," Hucklesbey said again laughing to himself at his own joke. "So tell me. What do you want to know about Mondomour?" Hucklesbey asked.

"Like I said before, what about his past? What was he like as a child? I mean, was he always evil or did something happen to make him the way he is? Why does he resent my grandfather so much?" Walt said wondering if he should say anything more.

"To be honest, I didn't really know him as a child so I can't help you there," Hucklesbey said taking a bite of the pizza they had ordered. "What I do know is that long ago, back in the time when your grandfather was first becoming well known as a mage, he and Mondomour spent a lot of time together." Hucklesbey paused a moment. "It wasn't until Merlin was asked to become Arthur's personal guard that things started to get ugly between Mondomour and your grandfather."

Walt cut him off. "What do you mean they spent time together? Were they friends? And what is this about being Arthur's personal guard?" Walt said having trouble making sense of everything.

"Well as I was saying your grandfather and Mondomour spent almost every day together I would assume they were very good friends but it soon changed due to Arthur asking the two most powerful mage's in the city to face off but he was only planning to see which of the two had the most power. Whoever did was welcomed into his castle as his royal guard. Now I know that sounds like slavery however Arthur knew as king he needed someone with magic blood on his side in order to protect him from his enemies" Hucklesbey said finishing the last of his pizza.

"So, you're telling me that before they were asked to fight and being the only two who were the most powerful they were like best friends? before this fight for Arthur?" Walt said starting to understand still very surprised.

"Yes exactly Mondomour wanted to serve Arthur more than anything in the world, my guess is because he wanted Arthur to eventually seize power and over throw the king" Hucklesbey replied. "As turns out your grandfather beat him and therefore was given the honor of Arthur's royal mage. This made Mondomour extremely jealous and envious of your grandfather, he soon let those feelings pass. As time went on Mondomour lurked around the castle almost daily begging Arthur to let him prove himself in other ways but Arthur just laughed and said that he could never measure up to Merlin's stature. This made Mondomour angry but he still wouldn't give up. Soon Merlin was spending almost every night up in his tower in Arthurs castle making something for Arthur using his powerful magic" Hucklesbey took a drink of water and continued. "Mondomour soon found out that Merlin was creating that medallion you now have around your neck" Hucklesbey said pointing to the medallion dangling from Walt's neck. "After being rejected by Arthur and finding out that Merlin had created that medallion Mondomour vowed he would kill Merlin and his family no matter how great a relative" Hucklesbey said with a disgusted look on his face. It took Walt a few minutes to take in everything he was hearing.

"So this is the reason why he wants to kill me? Because Merlin is my grandfather" Walt found it unfair his family was being singled out and going to have to suffer until Mondomour's dying day because of the medallion and other events from his grandfathers past.

"I can't believe it either, your family has been the target of Mondomour for many years and the only way it will stop is if you or a member of your family puts an end to his dark evil ways soon. Before you or someone else in your family is put in serious danger!" Hucklesbey said giving Walt a worried look. "Mondomour thought it unfair how your grandfather had created a magical object with so little effort, so he tried himself many times to replicate that medallion failing every time."

"So when did he find that it keeps whoever wears it immortal?" Walt asked.

"Well when Arthur was brought back from battle supposedly dead or mortally wounded Mondomour somehow found out" Hucklesbey answered.

"So Arthur had this medallion too?" Walt asked raising his eyebrows.

"Not for too long but yes he used it a few times although he didn't know of its power," Hucklesbey said grinning.

"So how did my grandfather keep the medallions power a secret from the king?"

"Well unfortunately Arthur was killed soon after the medallion was taken back by Merlin," Hucklesbey said in a sad voice.

"But why would my grandfather do that I thought he lived to serve Arthur?" Walt asked.

"Your grandfather thought it best that the medallion was kept within your family, he was afraid that someone other than himself would catch on to its true power. So shortly after your parents married the medallion was passed down to your father. He was told to keep it on him at all times until the day when his oldest child was old enough to receive it," Hucklesbey said rising from the table. The main reason why your grandfather did not mention the medallion's true power to Arthur is because he was afraid that if he did Arthur would want to rule England forever," Hucklesbey said keeping his voice low as they moved towards the door. Merlin was afraid that if he allowed Arthur to rule forever using the medallion's power the people living in England at the time would soon grow tired of his way of leading them and enforcing laws," Walt said surprised at himself for being able to figure that out.

"Exactly!" Hucklesbey said happy to know that Walt was actually still paying attention. They were outside once again. "I expect you understand that if you conceive a child you will have no choice but to entrust them with the medallion as soon as he/she is old enough?" Hucklesbey said giving Walt a serious look.

"Of course I understand but I'm not sure if that will even happen just yet Walt said. "Thank you for lunch and that information" Walt said as he began to leave.

"Anytime your highness it was my pleasure, I hope things work out for you and Elza" Hucklesbey said bowing slightly to Walt. "If you're in France for long call me if you have any more questions" Hucklesbey finished walking into the busy street and disappeared. Then Walt made his way across town dodging the oncoming traffic and many people.

Chapter 18
A Sudden Surprise

The next morning Walt awoke in his hotel room to find a letter on the bedside table. He picked up the letter and saw that it was from Elza. He almost forgot that he was in France. He turned over the envelope and tore it open. He took out the letter unfolded it and began reading the words aloud.

Dear Walt, I know that we had a fight and the words I said to you were unrespectable. I know this sounds too much like a queen, I'm not saying that you don't understand their meaning; I just mean that I didn't mean to be rude to you. I regret doing what I did. I hope you feel the same. I'm asking you this out of my love for you come home please. I am very sad and worried without you. I also have a surprise for you. I haven't told anyone yet and without you here I don't know how I can be happy about the news I have for you. Love Elza.

Walt finished reading the letter and decided that he would leave for home immediately. He packed his things, ran down to the front desk checked out and ran outside. He called Ickaris, got on his back, told him to fly home to the castle. They flew into the air and headed back toward home. Walt felt his heart leap and start to pound very fast at the thought of Elza's surprise. He was so excited that he almost fell off of Ickaris' back. Soon Walt knew they were close to home. When the city and Big Ben came into view. They landed and Walt jumped off of Ickaris' back and ran into the throne room.

"Good day your majesty" said a guard to Walt as he ran in.

"Hello" Walt said panting for breath. "Have you seen Elza today?" he asked.

"Yes I believe she is up in your royal sleeping quarters," he replied. He thanked the guard then ran up the staircase to their bedroom. He opened the door quietly and saw that Elza was asleep on the bed. He walked over to her quietly and nudged her with his hand.

"Elza" he whispered softly. "I'm home." Her eyes opened slowly and a smile appeared on her face. She got up and hugged him to her happy to have him home again.

"Never leave me like that again," she cried as she squeezed him.

"I won't I promise," Walt said. "What do you need to tell me?" he asked her smiling. She looked into his eyes and took a deep breath.

"I'm pregnant!" Elza said happily. "You and I are going to be parents!" she said hugging him again. "I hope you are happy about the news" Elza replied.

" I couldn't be more pleased" answered Walt.

Chapter 19
Spreading the News

That's wonderful news everyone told Elza and Walt together as they sat around the supper table eating a meal together as an entire family in the royal dining room. Both Elza and Walt's mothers were crying happily from the news.

"I just can't believe my little boy is growing up and is going to be a father," Walt's mother said to Elza's mother.

"My little girl is going to be a mother!" Elza's mother squealed in reply.

"Do you know what it is yet?" Walt asked Elza.

"A girl," she said smiling. "So we need to think of some good names for girls," she told him.

"Urn well since you've told me I've been thinking it over and I think maybe something with an S," Walt said.

"We need the book of names?" Elza said to him. "Mum where is the book of names?" Elza asked her mother.

"In the library dear," her mother replied smiling at Elza and Walt.

"Let's go then," Walt said taking Elza's hand. They walked briskly to the end of the castle heading for the library hand in hand.

Chapter 20
The Perfect Name

Soon Walt and Elza were sitting in the castle library with a very large book of names open in front of them.

"A name with an S, well there's Sandy, Samantha, Susan, Sally," Elza said going down the list with a finger and saying each name aloud to Walt. "Not good enough," Elza said voicing her opinions of each name aloud. "I think that her name needs to be unique. For she's not only a princess but a witch too.

"Well there are not many unique names with an "S" as the first letter in here." Walt replied. Then they heard someone coming down the aisle toward them.

"Any luck yet?" Walt's father asked as he was peeking around a book shelf.

"No dad not yet" said Walt.

"Well let me help" Walt's father asked coming toward the table.

"Dad can we do this alone?" Walt replied. "After all we are the baby's parents".

"Oh all right" Walt's father replied disappointedly.

"Sir we know that you want to help but we would like to do this on our own" Elza said.

"Yes, I understand I was the same way when Walt was born" Walt's father replied.

"Thanks dad" Walt called out as his father left the room.

"Oh here I love this one" Elza replied excitedly.

Walt looked at the name where Elza's finger was pointing. It read "Sophea." It says that this name represents, passion, peace and love." Walt said shaking his head in agreement.

"Yes I like this name too." Walt agreed. They were both happy that they finally agreed on a very unique and beautiful name for their new daughter. Then they put the big book of names back in its shelf and walked out of the library in high hopes for the coming of Princess Sophea. They exited the library and told their parent's the name for their baby.

"That's a beautiful name for a girl" said Elza's mother.

Walt and Elza decided not to tell the city about Sophea just yet. They would keep everything about the baby to themselves until the appropriate time.

Chapter 21
Mondomour's Interference

"A new baby!" "Oh that is BLOODY wonderful!" said Mondomour's evil voice.

"But sir" said one of Mondomour's servants. "That means that Walt will pass down the medallion when the baby is born". "I know bloody well what that means!" Mondomour yelled. "We need to stop this from happening, what do you suggest? Your evilness?" asked his servant.

"An ambush around the castle then I will go in and kill Elza!" Mondomour laughed.

"But you know that Walt will stop you before you get to her" said the servant.

"What did you just say?" Mondomour said grabbing the goblins throat "Nothing your evilness" Mondomour let go and he coughed gasping for breath.

"Goldor don't ever make me have to do that again!" Mondomour said in his raspy voice.

"Sorry master" replied Goldor meekly.

"Quiet all right" Mondomour said hitting Goldor on the shoulder. "Now you I wouldn't be just that obvious" Mondomour told Goldor. "What do you mean?" said Goldor the goblin.40

"Well first I will have my sister mix a poisonous elixir disguised as perfume which Elza will spray on herself and then soon feel the coldness of death come over her" said Mondomour. "You have a sister?" asked Goldor.

"Why yes, her name is Uvelda" said Mondomour proudly. "She is an expert at concocting poisons and other potions used for evil." "and I shall write to her now" Mondomour said excitedly. He ran to the top tower of his castle and quickly wrote a letter to his sister. He gave the letter to a black bat. Then said "take this to my sister in the woods to the north." The bat gave a screech and flew off the window edge and was swallowed up into the blackness of the night sky.

"The deed is done and soon all of England will be mine!" he laughed. Then he walked out of the tower in very high spirits with an evil smile all over his evil face.

Chapter 22
The Wedding

It was a hot sunny day in London, the early risers were just stepping out for their morning papers and a hot cup of coffee.

"Elza wake up!" Walt said as he rose from their bed. "Today's the day!" he said happily. Walt went down to the dining room for breakfast and sat at the table.

"Good morning your majesty what would you like for breakfast this morning?" asked Edgar the head butler.

"Oh how about some waffles and bacon with lots of maple syrup and a big glass of milk" Walt replied.

"All right I'll have the chefs get on that right away sir, is there anything else?" Edgar asked turning back to Walt.

"No that'll do for now" Walt said. "Edgar I was wondering have the chefs begun any preparations for this evening?" he said looking back at Edgar.

"Why yes sir, I believe that the chefs are making all of Elza's and your favorites and as far as decorating goes I believe we have just about finished with everything.

The guest list is in order as well" the butler said smiling at him.

"Good and one more thing Edgar I want the guards and anyone helping today to know that if they see any sign of Mondomour or his followers that they should notify me right away. I also would like the city heavily guarded as well." he said finally letting the butler head down to the kitchens that were underneath the castle. Walt waited a few minutes and soon Edgar and the head chef Pierre came up from the kitchens.

"Here is your breakfast sir enjoy" said Pierre setting a plate piled high with hot waffles and many strips of crispy bacon in front of Walt along with his big glass of milk and a container of syrup.

"Thank you" Walt said smiling at them both. Then the butler and the head chef left Walt alone to eat in peace. Walt ate silently and after a few minutes he seen Elza come in to sit with him.

"Good morning darling" he said as she took a seat. "Hungry?" he asked her.

"Not now" she replied. They both sat and talked about how excited they were for the day's events.

"I can't believe that this is actually happening!" Elza said excitedly. We're getting married today!

"I know" Walt replied smiling at her. Hours passed and soon everything was going according to plan. Decorations were hung, huge tables were placed in the ball room for the evenings feast. Elza was being chased around by her mother who was yelling at her due to a disagreement they had about the way Elza should wear her hair under her wedding Vail. Elza's mother was probably the most nervous for her daughter's big day. Walt decided that he would head down to the kitchens to see what sort of dishes were being prepared before getting ready.

"Pierre may I have a quick look at what is being prepared for tonight's meal?" he asked the head chef.

"Of course sir, I shall make it quick because it looks like you haven't gotten ready yet." Pierre said giving Walt a look of pity. "Don't you realize how important this day is to queen Elza. It's only a few hours away but not to worry all will be done in a jiffy" the head chef said moving along through the kitchen very quickly. Walt was shown many different dishes of all sorts of food definitely fit for a king. There were puddings, custards, stews, chickens and many different varieties of rice's, potatoes and thousands of other foods that looked and smelled wonderful.

"I better let you go get ready, good luck sir I hope everything is to your liking?" The chef said pushing him out of the kitchen and back up the stairs. "Thank you Pierre" Walt said turning quickly back to the chef then hurrying up the stairs to get changed. Before going to get ready Walt went out to the royal gardens and saw Elza sitting by the fountain. "How are you?" he said sitting down beside her. Silence came to them for a moment then Elza looked up at him.

"I can't wait anymore, we need to be married now!" she said sounding as if it would never happen.

"Don't worry I know it seems like forever but we will be married soon and then we all can be a true family." He said looking at Elza compassionately. "How is she?" he asked patting Elza's stomach. He felt Elza's breathing and the baby's kicking against his hand and it made him grin joyously.

"She's been fussy but at least I know she's there" Elza said smiling at Walt.

"Good that's wonderful" he replied kissing her on the cheek and getting up to go back inside the castle. Hours passed and soon Walt and Elza were taken to go get changed into their clothes for the wedding. Walt's father, Merlin and Elza's father took him to make sure everything was okay with his clothes and Walt's mother went with Elza's mother to help with Elza's dress.

"Ready son?" his father asked him as he looked at his son who was dressed in fancy clothes staring into a mirror at his reflection making sure everything was perfect.

"I think as ready as I can ever be!" he replied to his father.

"I'll be going to sit down then, good luck grandson" Merlin said smiling back at him as he left the dressing room. Walt's father wished him luck, hugged him and left shortly after Merlin and then Walt was told by Edgar to go to the

Abbey where everything would take place. As soon as he arrived he was told by the priest to wait at the front of the aisle for Elza. Photographers began snapping pictures and soon the church was filled with people. Walt finally made it to the front of the aisle and stood waiting for Elza his heart nearly jumping out of his chest. After what seemed like hours of millions of people staring and smiling and not to forget Walt and Elza's mothers' sobbing. Trumpets and drums began to play. Everyone stood and turned their heads. Walt looked up as the big oak doors at the front of the church opened. Elza came slowly walking through the doors along with her father who had his arm through hers looking straight ahead and smiling. Elza was wearing a big white wedding dress and her hair was pulled away from her face brought back in a spiky ponytail. The whole time she looked at Walt and smiled, he looked back grinning happily. Her father held her arm tightly as if fearing every moment of this day. He finally let her go kissed her on the cheek then with his wife and Walt's parents. The music stopped all went quite as the priest began the ceremony. Elza and Walt were now facing each other their eyes staring back at one another lovingly.

"Dearly beloved we are gathered here today to witness one of the most wonderful things that could ever happen. Two people deeply in love with one another being taken by the hands of God our heavenly father and being brought before him to this alter to be joined as one in the sacrament of holy matrimony. Now I gladly ask you Walter do you take Elza this woman to be your wife. To have, hold and cherish as your wife until death do you part?" The priest asked him looking to Walt. The church was silent and Walt took a deep breath.

"I do" he replied smiling at Elza and the priest.

"Then repeat after me, Elza I give you this ring" the priest said waiting for Walt to repeat. He repeated happily. "As a symbol of our love and my marriage to you. I ask you to accept this ring and become my wife" the priest said looking to Walt again. He repeated every word and placed the ring on Elza's left ring finger. "Now I turn to you" the priest said looking towards Elza. "Do you Elza take Walter this man to be your husband. To have, hold and cherish as your husband until death do you part?" Elza you may now place the ring on Walt's finger repeating after me. Once the rings were exchanged they could continue on with the rest of the ceremony. The priest asked this time waiting for Elza to respond. Again silence filled the church and Elza said with tears in her eyes.

"I do."

"Than by the power within me and all of England as our witnesses I pronounce you man and wife." The priest announced happily. Everyone cheered and music filled the church once again. "You may kiss the bride said the priest turning to Walt and he bent toward Elza and kissed her. All were happy once again and everyone in the city now saw how much Walt and Elza actually cared for each other on this their very happy wedding day.

Chapter 23
The Feast

After the ceremony everyone gathered in the large dining hall for supper. There were more than one-thousand guests flooding into the hall and scrambling to get a seat next to the king and queen.

"Where on earth did all of these people come from?" Walt exclaimed. "Well I know many of these people were not on the list" Walt said as he raised his wand to his throat. His voice echoed off of the walls and made everyone except Elza jump. "Attention everyone my wife and I appreciate and thank you all from the bottom of our hearts for wanting to help us enjoy our special day but this feast was only meant for our family not the entire city." Walt said looking to all of the people who were now frozen in fear looking up at him. Walt lowered his wand and the uninvited people were about to leave when Elza spoke.

"But now that you all are here we have decided to let you all stay in order to continue to help us eat all this delicious looking food and enjoy what is left of our wedding day."

"What?" Walt said looking at Elza surprised.

"You don't want to be seen as a bad king do you?" she asked him giving him a sad puppy dog face.

"Well I guess your right I just wasn't expecting the entire city of London to show up!" Walt replied. He then sat at the head of the table with Elza beside him and began eating. Soon the hall erupted in conversation, then Walt and Elza's parents along with Walt's grandfather stood and everyone became silent again. When Walt's father began to speak the talking subsided.

"My wife and I would like to purpose a toast" he told the crowded hall as he and his wife rose their wine glasses.

"We would like to toast to our son the new king of England and our new daughter - in - law Elza we are very happy that these two came across each other and hope that together they will build an unbreakable relationship and a strong family together. As they become happy we do too" he said together with his wife. Everyone raised their glasses to the new happy couple then cheered. Then Elza's parents took their turn.

"We would also like to toast to our daughter and new son - in - law, we hope that they continue what kings and queens before them have done and keep England safe for all. Not only that but also keep each other happy until the day they part in death." Elza's mother said smiling at them. They sat down but Merlin remained standing.

"I know these types of speeches can get pretty long especially when your daughter and son in law are the new ruler's of this country." Merlin said smiling at the queen then everyone laughed at his joke. "But I just wanted to say these two have trained

together. He said looking at Walt and Elza, "over the past few years with me as their teacher they have not only learned from me but I also have learned a great deal from them. Although I hate to admit it I never knew at first that these two had begun a relationship together that is until they arrived at my academy. From then on I knew that they would someday be married and also learned how old I really was," the crowd laughed again and he continued. "I guess when one has so many things they wish to accomplish they lose track of where their life has gone and suddenly before they know it everything comes at them in a surprising way. I also kept the secret of Elza being a princess from my grandson and wish now that I could've told him earlier but in light of what happened since they first started training with me I forgot and let the years pass. I wish to congratulate this new beautiful couple and also wish to be forgiven for not sharing the truth with you Walt that is until a few months ago" Merlin said smiling at them and taking a seat. Everyone clapped and Walt and Elza stood. Once again everyone was quiet.

"Thank you all for being here" Walt said looking at the people to each side of him. "We are very pleased that you all decided to come and I would like to say I'm sorry about what I said earlier it was rude and I am grateful that you all are here no matter who you are, I will now allow my wife to add a few words before we all go back to eating this wonderful food." he said turning to Elza.

"Thank you dear" she said smiling at him and turning towards the people before her. "As we all have said a lot this day we really do thank you all for coming and hope that you are enjoying the food and having a wonderful time, having all of you here means the world to us we would not ask to change it one bit. Walt and I now would like to purpose a toast to our parents and Walt's grandfather." Elza said raising her glass with Walt and taking a breath. "Mum and dad thank you for supporting me even when I wasn't at home in the castle and I also wanted to say thank you for letting Walt take your little girl away from you. I promise you both that he will keep me safe and protect me as well as he can" she went and hugged her parents then sat down again.

"I want to thank my parents and my grandfather who have been there for me whenever I have needed them in the good times and bad. Also I want to extend a thank you to those of you who have helped my grandfather by teaching Elza and I when he was busy without your help we would never have understood the things that happen in the magical world we live in today. It is an amazing place and those who help keep it that way deserve a big hand" he went and hugged his mother and shook his father's and grandfather's hand then went back to sit down smiling at her. "Good night dear," Walt said and he leaned over beside Elza and finished eating. They all sat and talked as soon as the meal was complete, soon their wonderful eventful day had ended the tables and decorations were cleared from the dining hall and various rooms that had been used around the castle.

"Today was the greatest day of my life" Elza said to Walt as they sat up in their bed that evening.

"Mine too," Walt replied and kissed her.

"Good night," she said softly. Then they fell asleep and dreamed of their life together and a long road ahead that they would travel down together.

Chapter 24
The Reply

"Mondomour a letter has come for you!" Goldor said running to him.

"Give that to me!" he snapped the letter from Goldor's hand. He tore open the letter and read it to himself. Then he took a black bottle out of the envelope.

"What does it say?" Goldor asked trying his best to get a glimpse at the letter.

"None of your business now go away!" Mondomour yelled. He then ran to one of the dark wizards who had become part of his army. "Carefully take this to Walt tell him it is a late wedding present for the queen from a close friend." Mondomour said looking down at the little man standing before him.

"I'll need a disguise" said the dark wizard in reply.

"Hold still" Mondomour said raising his wand. Suddenly the small dark wizard was transformed into an old sales man.

"Will I be able to change back?" the dark wizard asked now fully transformed.

"Yes this transformation is temporary" Mondomour replied. "You must deliver this quickly before you change back" Mondomour finished sending him on his way.

Chapter 25
A Present for the Queen

S oon the disguised dark wizard reached the city and the castle gate.

"Do you have an appointment to see the king or queen, old beggar?" the guard at the gate asked.

"I was sent with a gift for queen Elza," the dark wizard replied trying his best to sound and act the part.

"Whom may I ask is it from?" the guard questioned suspiciously.

"Whom I do not know the dark wizard said keeping as straight a face as he could.

"Well I cannot let you pass then!" the guard said fiercely.

"Please I am a mere salesperson, may I suggest to have someone deliver what I was sent here with to the king?" the dark wizard pleaded.

"Wait here" the guard replied then making his way into the castle.

"Mondomour!" the dark wizard said then a voice echoed through his thoughts.

"Yes what is it?" Mondomour's voice echoed back. "The guard left me outside the gate and went to get Walt but if I wait any longer the spell will wear off" the dark wizard said in a worried voice.

"Then squeeze through a gap someplace and run to a window and climb in, then get to their bedroom and set the bottle on the nightstand and get out of their before anyone catches you!" Mondomour's voice screamed back.

"All right sir I'll do my best" the dark wizard said quickly running around the outside gate in the hopes that he would find a way into the castle.

"Hey" Mondomour's voice called.

"Yes sir what is it?" the dark wizard replied finally getting over the gate and onto the other side.

"What is your name?" Mondomour's voice asked. "Morlock sir" the dark wizard replied.

"Ah okay then, Morlock if you succeed you shall be rewarded" Mondomour's voice called back happily.

"I will not fail you sir" Morlock replied. Then he quickly proceeded to the king and queens bedroom window and made his way up the side using a grappling hook he happened to have with him. Soon he was standing in the royal bedroom where he placed the little black bottle on the nightstand and disappeared. The guard came back to the gate.

"He's gone" the guard said to Walt who was making his way out of the castle.

"He must have gotten tired of waiting," Walt replied turning back to the castle entrance. "Did he tell you why he had the gift?" Walt asked.

"No your majesty, he did seem suspicious like something wasn't right about him or like he was hiding something. That's why I came to get you sir," the guard said being honest.

"Search the castle, look for something that you know shouldn't be within these walls," Walt said telling the guard to notify every other guard to do the same before a problem resulted.

"Right away your highness," the guard said saluting to Walt.

"Honey what is this?" Elza asked Walt as he came through the castles front doors. She held out the black bottle of poison in front of him.

"Give it here" Walt said looking at the black bottle suspiciously. She handed him the bottle. "This needs to go to my grandfather immediately and then he can examine the contents and tell us what it is." Walt said running for his grandfather who was up in one of the castles top towers.

He came to the top steps and knocked on the door, he was told to enter so he opened the door. "Grandfather take a look at this" Walt said showing Merlin the tiny black bottle. "Do you have any idea what it could be? Elza found it in our room. "I was told by the guards outside the castle that there was a suspicious looking man who came to them claiming that he had a gift for the queen and I think this is what they wanted to get to us. Only the guards said that the man wouldn't tell them what the gift was or who it came from!" Walt said frantically as he handed the bottle to his grandfather. Merlin slowly opened the bottle and sniffed it just a bit.

"Poison!" Merlin said closing the bottle again.

"How do you know?" Walt asked looking surprised.

"Walt I have had to deal with situations like this many times before." Merlin said looking at Walt like he should have known that. "I actually was almost killed by a poison disguised like this once but thankfully I had that medallion," Merlin said looking to the medallion around Walt's neck. "We need to find out who created this and whoever that man got it from and then an arrest will have to be made! "Merlin said going back to his work.

"Understood, I will get that done this evening!" Walt responded.

"Thank you for coming to me," Merlin said turning back to Walt.

"I would any time there is suspicion or if something like this happens again." Walt said smiling at Merlin. "I will be back" he said as he left the tower." Walt told the guards that he had wanted to have a meeting in the room where the round table sat. Then he rounded up his knights and they entered the room and took seats at the table. "Now that I have all of you here know that as your new king this is my first major meeting with all of you and I would like to discuss our first plan of action!" Walt said looking at everyone around the table. "We need to settle these quarrels with Mondomour, I have reason to believe that someone working for him was sent to the castle in order to insure that my wife received a special "gift" Walt said. "It is a good thing we all acted fast otherwise my wife could have been killed!" Walt said taking a moment to think. "This may not be okay with any of you or let alone the others of the city. But I have decided to end this once and for all by taking us to war. Believe me this is not something I wanted to do but to be honest this country has been in this war for many years without anyone taking serious action or even realizing what is happening." Walt looked once again around the table allowing his knights and guards to voice their opinions. No one said a word so he continued. "Many people have had to suffer and lots have been killed because of what Mondomour is doing, however, I feel that if something isn't done now things will only get worse. I want someone to make contact with any other country willing to help us destroy this problem. Also I want security increased around the castle. Training will start immediately for every knight available to me. I expect all of you to work as a team out there on the battlefield and help not only this castle but all of England to win this war and regain peace!" Walt said leaning back in his chair. "You are all dismissed" Walt finished. Then everyone got up and left Walt sitting alone at the round table to think about what he had just told them.

Chapter 26
The Never Ending Battle

"Why are you doing this?" Elza asked Walt after hearing his plan.

"Because Mondomour has gone too far, he could've killed you had you used the poison. He has a big army and if we don't fight back we'll lose the castle and England." Walt said sitting on his throne watching Elza walk back and forth in front of him. "As king I need to do my job and that means anytime there is a problem I need to take some form of action to handle it." Walt said trying to get Elza to understand him.

"Well as queen I need to agree with you and so far I don't agree!" Elza replied raising her eyebrows "In order to make it through this we need to agree and by disagreeing we won't accomplish anything!" she said sitting beside him. Please don't make people die Walter." Elza pleaded with him.

"First of all just because I demand that this country go to war does not mean I want or force people to die, and secondly I can't just tell the knights to stop training otherwise they will think I don't want to save the country." Walt retorted back at her.

"I'm not saying that you want people to die or that you don't care for the country but you have already proven your loyalty to more than this country. I just don't think that going to war is the best step to take." Elza told him taking his hand in hers.

"The baby is coming in a few days and you know as well as I do that if Mondomour isn't put to an end now he will come and try to kill her or all of us." Walt said with a worried look on his face. "This is in God's hands now, I've done all I can." Walt said looking up to the ceiling.

"War will come if he feels that is the right thing to do! Walt said getting up from his throne.

"Promise me that you won't get yourself killed." Elza whispered as she walked up behind him.

"I promise." Walt replied then he kissed her. "I must go check on the knights." he said then he walked out to the courtyard. "We move to battle tonight!" Walt called to all his

knights as he paced back and forth in front of them. "You all have done very well during these past few weeks of training, although it may not be your best it is up to each and every one of you to fight with everything you've got!" Walt said forcefully. "Remember to battle as a team, you will follow only my orders and also remember there is no turning back!" Walt said going up and down the line of knights and looking at them all one by one. "We fight until the end!" He said ending his orders. The knights took a bow to Walt and then held up their swords.

"All hail king Walter!" the group said as one and then cheering erupted from them all echoing through the castles windows. The sky darkened as evening drew closer and once again Walt was standing before his knights. This time both Elza, Merlin and both Elza and Walt's parents along with Ickaris Walt's dragon joined the group.

"The hour is upon us!" Walt said before everyone. "Now before we go into battle we shall take a moment to pray to our lord God!" Walt said bowing his head. Everyone joined hands and began to pray.

"Dear God our Heavenly father all of us standing before you pray that all will go well in the midst of battle, keep all of us safe from harm. If we fall we ask that you keep Mondomour away from England and our families. We realize that not all of us standing here will make it back but will perish on the battlefield in war. We hope that those who give their lives for the protection of this kingdom and this country will be welcomed into your castle to join you and the rest of the angels in eternal life and be at peace in your Heaven. Protect us dear father thank you and may your name be praised forever more Amen." Everyone said together. Then Walt climbed up onto Ickaris's back and told Elza that he loved her. He leaned down and kissed her.

"Be careful and come home to me," she whispered to him. He nodded his head and Elza patted Ickaris on the side gazing into his large golden eyes. Then he flew into the air motioning to his men to follow and they marched off. Walt didn't look back for he knew it would only increase the pain of having to leave the castle and Elza behind. He also knew that although she had tried not to show it Elza had tears in her eyes.

Chapter 27
A Bloody Battle

Walt and his band of knights stopped along the way to gather the soldiers that had agreed to help fight against Mondomour. Darkness filled the air and Walt knew that they were close.

"We are getting closer!" Walt yelled down to them descending a little. "On my signal!" Walt said to the archers that were readying their bows and arrows seeing Mondomour's army as they came over a hill. Walt signaled to the archers to fire. Their arrows sliced through the air and came down on Mondomour and his army. Shrieks of death and pain filled the air. Walt drew Excalibur and flew closer to the swarm of the dark army, his many knights followed suit soon the sparks of wands were flying through the air and swords clashed. Walt dodged the spells as he flew right at Mondomour. Excalibur was pointed straight out in front of him gleaming in the last light of day

"*Evica Lomorum*" Mondomour yelled drawing his wand aiming it right at Walt once he saw him coming at him. Walt blocked the curse with his sword laughing at Mondomour knocking him onto the ground.

"You are the one who will die today!" Walt said through clenched teeth as jumped in front of Mondomour from his dragons back.

"Ah but you should know yourself Walter that a wand is much more powerful than a sword even if it is sacred" Mondomour said smiling up at him.

"I don't intend to kill you today only take you as my prisoner for now." Walt replied holding his swords point to Mondomour's throat. "Guards take him away!" called Walt keeping his eyes on Mondomour. Before Mondomour could do anything the knights were around him. They tied him up and the rest of his army was destroyed. "Take him to the castle dungeon. I will have an executioner brought to the castle as soon as we return!" Walt said as his knights took Mondomour away. " This war is not over until this man before us is dead!" Walt said getting back onto Ickaris's back soaring into the air. They arrived back at the castle and everyone was astonished at how Walt had managed to capture Mondomour in such little time. Merlin stared in amazement at his grandson as he came in through the front doors.

(he has done what I and many kings' before him could not.) Merlin thought smiling.

"Mondomour shall be executed at dawn tomorrow morning!" Walt said to his people shortly after returning from battle. Everyone around the castle cheered and watched as Mondomour was taken to the castles dungeon. "You're safe now" Walt told Elza as he entered the castle again. "Sophea can come in peace now." he said smiling at her.

"That's wonderful!" Elza said kissing him. "How did you catch him after all this time?" she asked.

"I caught him off guard." Walt said smiling.

"But What if he escapes again?" Elza asked looking worried.

"He won't the jail cell he is placed in and the entire dungeon is enclosed with a magic enchantment that only my grandfather and I know he is trapped." Walt said walking down to the dungeon to make sure Mondomour was placed in a cell. Inside his cell there was only a bed made of straw in one of the corners, he had nothing else available to him. Walt walked around the cell eyeing Mondomour as he went. "How does it feel to be a prisoner in my castle?" Walt asked him still pacing around the cell. "How does it feel to know that by noon tomorrow you will be dead and that you have no one to help you escape?" Walt said trying not to laugh so he grinned broadly instead. "You lost Mondomour after all these years I have you right where I want you!" Walt said laughing now.

"That's it you little!" Mondomour said trying to lunge at him but he was thrown back as electricity shocked him.

"Like that little touch I added?" Walt asked. "This war between this country, my people and you is over!" Walt said looking at Mondomour who was sitting on the floor of his cell now.

"You think you've won but you haven't. I will return again like I did before, then I will kill every last one of your people and your family!" Mondomour said staring up at Walt evilly.

"Not without your wand or your magic you won't!" Walt finished turning his back on him as he strode out of the dungeon.

Chapter 28
Mondomour's Last Words

Everyone in London gathered around the castle and waited for the execution, even little children gathered in a group to watch. Mondomour was going to be hanged, he was brought to the platform where the executioner placed a rope around his neck. Walt came to the balcony with Elza and spoke to the people.

"You see the man that has caused misery and also has caused our country to break out into war he will die this day and will no longer be a burden on any of us!" Walt called out to the city's people e below him. Drums started playing and Mondomour was raised into the air. The executioner placed his hands on the ropes end and pulled. There was a loud crack and Mondomour's lifeless body dangled high in the air.

"The evil of this dark wizard is gone and now we can all live in peace." Walt called to the people who cheered loudly. "Take his body and lock it in a coffin and then bring it to me." Walt told the guards stationed outside the doors of the balcony. Soon the guards brought a black coffin into the throne room of the castle and placed it at Walt and Elza's feet. Then they both bowed and left the hall.

"What are you going to do now?" Elza asked him.

"Well just sit back and watch me," he replied drawing his wand. He pointed it directly at the coffin and said, "*Stoneorium!*"

"What did you do that for he's already dead?" Elza said giving Walt a suspicious look.

"Yes honey I know but this is to make sure he won't come back again." Walt said smiling at his wife. "Guards take this and melt it in the furnace down in the dungeon" Walt called to the guards standing outside the doors.

"Right away your majesties." said the guards preparing to take the stone encrusted coffin down to the furnace to be melted.

"Wait don't bother I'll take care of this." Merlin said coming into the throne room. He came into the throne room and stood over the coffin. He raised his hands and said, "*Vanilious!*" and the coffin turned to ash and disappeared. Then the evil of Mondomour the dark wizard that had plagued London for three years was gone.

Chapter 29
A New Princess

L ondon seemed safer now that Mondomour was dead, but the people didn't know about Uvelda Mondomour's sister. Who had taken the news of her brother's death very badly. She was overcome with anger.

"Oh dear God how could he have been so foolish to fall into their trap?" she asked herself "However I will avenge him and carry out what he could not. By stealing the new born princess and killing Merlin the one my brother hated the most!" she said again to herself. Back at the castle screams of pain filled the city it was dark and all the people were asleep. Except for Walt, his parents, Elza's parents, the royal attendants, Elza and Merlin. Sophea was coming into the world.

"Hang in there" said a royal attendant to Elza. "Almost there!" another said smiling to the queen. Soon the infants crying could be heard behind the infirmary's doors. Walt waited at the doors with Merlin and his father becoming even more anxious to see his new daughter.

"You may come in now and see" said an attendant peeking her head out through the doors. Walt stood looking at his new daughter smiling with tears in his eyes.

"Congratulations" Merlin said to Walt and Elza smiling
proudly at them. Walt then walked slowly up to Elza as she spoke to Sophea softly.

"Say hi to your daddy" she whispered. The baby made a face that everyone knew probably could have been a smile and they laughed happily. Then Sophea and Elza were taken into the nursery and they were finally left alone to rest

Chapter 30
A New Life

"How is she?" Walt asked Elza coming into the nursery smiling.

"She's doing just fine." Elza replied weakly.

"Are you okay ?" Walt asked her.

"Yes, I have some pains still though." she replied weakly smiling at him as he sat in the chair next to the bed.

"Need anything?" Walt asked coming over to her and stroking the side of her face gently with his hand.

"No not yet" Elza replied taking a breath. "She'll be a great princess" Elza said looking over at Sophea who was wrapped like a cocoon. "Yeah I hope so." Walt said sitting back down in the chair. "I have to give the medallion to Sophea when she's old enough." Walt told Elza.

"She'll enjoy having it." Elza said smiling. "Does this mean were getting old?" she asked looking at Walt with worry on her face.

"No nonsense why would you say that?" he asked her. "I don't know usually once you marry and have children it seems as if people get older faster" she said quietly.

"Well I don't expect to get old too soon." he said laughing a little. He picked up Sophea slowly, sat back down in the chair and began rocking her. "We now are a complete family," Walt said looking at Elza smiling.

Chapter 1
The Kidnapping

London hadn't changed much although five years had passed. Sophea was a little older but still not old enough to know what she was.

"Daddy can I go play with Siegfried?" Sophea asked running to her father.

"Yes but stay close to the castle." Walt said.

She was now five years old and she loved to go play with Siegfried. Siegfried was her best friend. His father was a blacksmith in the city. "I can't believe how much she has grown" Walt said to Merlin as his grandfather came into the throne room.

"Yes it's amazing how quick time passes by" Merlin replied smiling. "When will you tell her?" Merlin asked.

"Oh she's not nearly old enough yet" Walt said giving his grandfather a look of anger. "I didn't find out about my powers or you until I was fifteen." Walt added the anger rising in his tone.

"Well don't be like your parents tell her early before it is too late for me to train her" Merlin pleaded with sadness in his voice.

"Fine but Elza has to be here too when we tell Sophea about her power's." Walt said agreeing with his grandfather. "But you know that I am her father, I should decide when my daughter should know." Walt said.

"I guess you're right but know this my time here is running short." Merlin sighed to himself. "Old age is coming to me very quickly now and soon will death." Merlin added moving his gaze slowly to the floor.

"Oh come now grandfather it makes us sad when rumors of death lurk about." Walt replied moving towards his grandfather and gently patting him on the back.

"Sorry." Merlin said sadly.

"Where is Elza I haven't seen her all day?" Walt asked his grandfather changing the subject.

"She mentioned to me earlier that she was going to see her parents for a bit." Merlin replied.

"Oh she hadn't told me." Walt said going out to the royal gardens for a walk.

"Sophea wait for me!" Siegfried called as he ran after Sophea in the forest a great distance away from the castle. She ran fast with her light brown hair flowing behind her in the wind. Suddenly she collapsed then Uvelda ran out from behind a big pine tree and swept her up.

"Finally I have what I need to bring my brother back from the grave. Then all the power will be ours!"

Uvelda laughed. Siegfried stopped suddenly and hid behind a tree watching Uvelda disappear with Sophea unconscious in her arms. Siegfried began running to the castle as fast as he could. He sprinted through the city nearly out of breath finally coming to the castle gates. He was fast for a five year old.

"Open the gate!" He screamed at the guard. "The princess is in trouble!" Siegfried cried out as he ran into the throne room. Walt ran to Siegfried in a rush clutching him trying to calm him down.

"What happened?" Walt asked the horror stuck Siegfried. "Siegfried you must tell me what has happened to my daughter?" Walt said again as Siegfried sobbed. Tears came rolling down the little boy's cheeks as he took a deep breath.

"I'm sorry sir but a woman... She-she grabbed her and took - took her" he said as he started sobbing again.

"A woman? Who?" Walt asked Siegfried looking straight into the sobbing boy's eyes. "What did she look like?" he said very frantic now.

Siegfried took a deep breath. "Black hair, she had a wand and wore a black tattered dress." He said wiping away his tears.

"Okay thank you my boy." Walt said letting him go. "Guards!" Walt yelled as he rose from the floor. "Track down Uvelda Mondomour's sister! She has kidnapped my daughter. Find her before she is harmed and bring her home." He told them running out to the court yard. "Merlin contact Elza and tell her to come home immediately. I'm going to my parents to tell them."

Walt called out to his grandfather as he rounded up all of the guards outside the castle. That was the first time in Merlin's life that he had taken a direct command from his grandson as surprised as he was to have realized this he obeyed without hesitation.

"But your highness how do you know it is Mondomour's sister? What if it is someone else?" One of the guards asked giving Walt a questioning look.

"There is only one woman in this entire city that ever wears black tattered dresses and kidnaps children! Yes I know it is her!" Walt yelled staring at the guard menacingly.

"Now do as I say and never question me again otherwise I will have you thrown out!" he yelled infuriated by the guard.

"Sorry my king." the guard said turning as white as a sheet and running after the others.

"Merlin is it true?" Elza asked the holographic image of Merlin hovering before her as she sat in the back of a limousine heading back to the castle.

"Yes? am afraid so /y tiieel is." Merlin's image replied back with worry in his voice. "Walt has sent the castle guards out to look for her." he said trying his best to remain calm. The limo stopped outside the royal courtyard of the castle and the driver got out of the car to quickly open the passenger door to let the queen out.

"Walter I want that bitch killed and my little girl back where she belongs!" Elza screamed as she came toward her husband in a fit of rage.

"No reporters are allowed in Walt called to the one guard standing at the gate.

"Yes your highness" He replied with a bow. Elza was sobbing as Walt escorted her back into the castle.

"I will do all I can to stop this and bring Sophea home safely" Walt said comforting her. Then he kissed her leaving immediately to go looking for Sophea.

Chapter 2
An Evil Reunion

"Where am I?" Sophea called into the candle lit room as she awoke. "Daddy?" she said as silence continued.

"My dear your daddy isn't here." Uvelda replied moving over to the side of the bed and looking down at Sophea wickedly.

"Who are you?" Sophea asked sitting up.

"Well that's not important right now is it?" Uvelda replied trying to keep herself from becoming angry. "Come here" Uvelda said turning to Sophea. Sophea then scooted herself to the edge of the bed and walked over to Uvelda. "Hold out your hand" Uvelda said to her. Sophea slowly raised her hand presenting it to Uvelda.

"Who are you" Sophea asked again.

"My dear I thought I told you not to worry about that!" Uvelda said angrily. "Now this will only hurt a bit" she told Sophea slowly raising a small knife and placing it on Sophea's wrist. Suddenly the door blasted open and Merlin along with Elza stormed in.

"Stop right there you old hag" Merlin shouted at Uvelda his wand pointed right at her. Sophea was quickly swept into Elza's arms and Sophea clutched her mother for dear life with tears in her eyes.

"How dare you take my daughter away from my husband and I" Elza screamed at her. Uvelda was silent with fear on her face. Then Merlin, Elza and Sophea disappeared with a crack leaving Uvelda standing once again in the silent room alone.

Soon Sophea was back at the castle, safe from harm. Walt had also returned.

"I don't understand why these things just won't stop happening and we can live a normal life," Walt said to Elza running his fingers through his hair in frustration.

"You know why Walt," Elza said looking at her husband with concern. "Uvelda thought that by taking Sophea she would be able to return Mondomour from the grave and then they would kill her," Elza replied.

"Why did I have to be cursed with this?" Walt said taking the medallion and holding it out in front of him. "We're suppose to give it to Sophea soon" Walt said looking at the medallion sadly. "I'm afraid if we do it will only cause more mayhem," Walt said worriedly.

"Walter it is the only right and it will protect her you know that." Elza told him.

"Well as long as I'm king no daughter of mine will be cursed by this medallion" Walt said putting the medallion in the pocket of his robe. "Grandfather bring Sophea from her room I think its time we tell her." Walt said as his grandfather descended the stairs to his tower. "We need to tell her Elza. Before things get to out of hand." Walt said looking toward her.

"Are you sure? Now?" Elza asked looking afraid.

"Yes now!" Walt said raising his eyebrows. Merlin held Sophea in his arms as he entered the throne room coming to Walt and Elza then setting her down at her parents' feet.

"Sophea your mother and I have something to tell you." Walt said to his daughter looking her right in the eyes.

"Yes what is it?" Sophea asked making a face at her father then looking at her mother with a questioning look. Walt reached into his robe pocket and pulled out the purple wooden wand he had been saving since the day of her birth.

"What your father is trying to say is that you are a witch." Elza replied smiling at her. Sophea's little mouth fell open in surprise. She ran to her parents hugging them then taking her wand and holding it out joyously.

"Now honey do you know what this is?"

Walt asked Sophea picking her up and holding her on his lap.

"Yes daddy I do" Sophea replied looking up at Walt excitedly. "But why?" she asked looking at the wand in her hands wonderingly.

"Sophea you along with me, your father and all the rest of our family have magic in our blood and it is necessary that you begin to understand what that means" Elza said turning to her daughter and smiling at her. A few days passed and Sophea was beginning to understand what her parents had said. Merlin began her training as well. Mondomour had returned with the help of his sister and evil settled back into the hearts of the entire city once again.

"What do we do now?" Walt asked Elza as they sat in their room one morning.

"Do what we've always done dear fight!" Elza replied looking worried for what might happen next.

"So be it." Walt said opening the door and walking down the hall to his daughter's room with sadness in his eyes.

Chapter 3
Mondomour Strikes Back

"It seems as if I was never gone." Mondomour said looking at his sister smiling.

"It is very good to have you back brother dear. I was beginning to think you could never return" Uvelda replied with a look of sadness on her face.

"Oh dear sister you are an expert in the dark arts and it is only right that I thank you for helping me return." Mondomour said giving his sister a sly smile.

"What do you mean?" Uvelda replied looking at him in confusion.

"My son Tom? with your magic you could..." Mondomour pleaded before his sister rudely cut him off.

"No way Mondomour are you insane!" Uvelda asked shouting at him. "I thought you killed the boy because you hated that he disobeyed you after he had agreed to help us get that medallion?" Uvelda said becoming enraged. "He's a lover of the king!" Uvelda said infuriated from having to think about her nephew.

"I know but who will take over if I ever die of old age?" Mondomour asked drumming his fingers on the table.

"Your son is dead, his place is somewhere else now!" Uvelda said calming down but still annoyed by what her brother was saying. "It was only right to do what you did, my nephew was a disgrace to the family name. He could never be as evil as you" Uvelda replied narrowing her eyes as if Tom were standing right before her.

"Leave my castle now!" Mondomour said through gritted teeth.

"What?" Uvelda said aghast.

"I said, GET THE BLOODY HELL OUT NOW!" Mondomour screamed at her turning red in the face his words echoing off the stone walls of his castle. He now was completely out of his chair and he had his wand out which was pointed right at his sister threateningly.

"But brother..." Uvelda said looking as if she were about to cry.

"NO BUTS! LEAVE NOW OR BE KILLED!" Mondomour said still infuriated with her clutching his wand tightly. Uvelda rose from her chair and disappeared without another word. Mondomour knew what he wanted to do, he wanted his son back. Not his son that loved but his son that he knew would help him and was entirely evil.

He only had the one son but he knew if he preformed the right magic he could easily get him to help him destroy England, kill Walt and all his family.

"Yes that's what I will do. Tom will return, be evil and help me get the medallion. Then when the time is right we will take the castle and rule for all eternity!" Mondomour said to himself laughing maniacally.

Chapter 4
The Resurrection

It was a foggy day in London. Mondomour trudged through the city in a black cloak his head covered with its hood. He soon came to the edge of the city and could see the headstone of his son's grave in the distance. A cool breeze swept across Mondomour's face. He knelt down in front of the headstone and withdrew his wand from inside his robe.

"Back away from the grave!" a voice said and Mondomour whipped around.

"Who's there?" he called into the silence looking every which way.

"Not to worry I've come only to warn you" the voice continued.

"Warn me of what Mondomour said laughing to himself.

"Only that you must never try to reawaken the dead once they have crossed into the next life." the voice finished.

"Show yourself bloody coward!" Mondomour shouted his voice echoing off into the distance. There was a sudden gust of wind and a whitish blue figure appeared right in front of Mondomour.

"Hello father" said Tom looking his father straight in the face. Mondomour sat staring horror struck into his son's transparent face.

"T-Tom is...is that you?" Mondomour asked stuttering in horror.

"Yes father it is and I have come here of my own free will to tell you that you cannot try to bring me back to life." Tom replied looking at his father with his eyebrows raised.

"Why is that?" Mondomour asked confused.

"Father it is too late, I've already gone into the afterlife and even with your plan to bring me back to get me to help you kill Walt and take the medallion. Not even his medallion could bring me back because it has been too long." Tom said. "What you did to me eight years ago can never be forgotten, now before I go I just want you to know as hard as it is for me to say this I love you and have no choice but to accept you for who you are no matter if you are evil or not." Tom said beginning to fade away. "Goodbye father, mum and I are watching over you every day and miss you very much. We wish that you would go away from darkness and become who you used to be." Tom said disappearing from view. Mondomour then sat thinking of what his son had said and then he rose to his feet and placed his wand back into his pocket. He was about to turn away when he turned back to the headstone and placed a dark red tulip beside it.

"Rest in peace my son." Mondomour said to himself with a tear in his eye and then he turned and walked away slowly.

Chapter 5
The New Apprentice

Walt and Elza were expecting the Prime Minister and sat waiting patiently in the throne room for him to arrive. "What are we going to do about Mondomour? He has been gathering our people and managing to get them to join him. If we don't do something soon he may try to kidnap Sophea again or worse take over the castle!" Walt said becoming nervous.

"Walt get a hold of yourself you and I have ruled England for six years now and Sophea will be fine. She has the medallion now that will help her stay safe." Elza replied calming her husband.

"I'm just worried we're missing something. I just don't understand how the hell he keeps coming back to life every time we kill him?" Walt asked giving Elza a questioning look. "I thought that was why he wanted the medallion. So that he could keep himself immortal and never have to worry about dying" Walt added making himself worry even more.

"Well Walt I think your over reacting, I know ruling a country and worrying about how the people feel along with protecting your family isn't easy but you have done things before that you thought you would never do." Elza said trying to keep control of Walt's feelings. "Do you remember that day when you stopped Mondomour for the first time?" Elza asked looking towards Walt.

"Yes," Walt replied.

"Well do you remember what General Tumzil said? How if we stand together and fight we will make it through everything," Elza said.

"Okay so maybe I am over reacting but I just don't want him hurting our daughter!" Walt replied angrily.

"Well that's why we have Merlin to help train her and watch over her." Elza said still calm.

"Elza you know as well as I do that my grandfather won't be around forever!" Walt said anger still in his voice.

"I do but for now..." Elza began but Walt interrupted her.

"For now we need to start being like real parents and protect our daughter." Walt said making Elza frown a little. One of the castles guards came striding up the aisle toward them.

"Your graces, the Prime Minister is here to speak with you now," the guard said bowing to them.

"Send him in," Walt told the guard.

"Yes sir." He took another bow and left the throne room.

"Your Majesties," the Prime Minister said as he came into the throne room giving them a bow."I expect you know why I am here." The Prime Minister said eyed them both and continued. "I understand that the events of the past years have brought about a major war and we have not had much time to discuss a possible way out."

"Prime Minister, as Queen I see this issue as a means of distraction and a way for Mondomour to begin to take out his plans to over throw my husband and I. Then take position as king," Elza replied stating her opinion.

"My lady, you are right but what do you propose I do since I don't have any magic in me I don't see how much help I will actually be to you both." the Prime Minister said looking sad.

"Well in the past Mondomour has tried numerous times to take what he truly wants which happens to be something I posses." Walt replied speaking up. "I became king only a few years ago and I feel that the only reason why Mondomour wants the throne is because I am king and I have what he truly wants!" Walt added.

"What exactly is that?" the Prime Minister asked confused after a minute.

"If I told you I would endanger my family but I will say the thing he wants has power beyond the likes of anything else!" Walt said with a stern look on his face. The Prime Minister beamed at Walt with eyes wide then spoke.

"I do however have news about a new apprentice Mondomour has acquired." the Prime Minister said happily. Walt and Elza eyed the Prime Minister intently.

"Anything more" Elza asked.

"Yes as you both know being as you were both there" the Prime Minister said looking at them with eagerness. "His new apprentice at least he hopes will follow him and does as he does." the Prime Minister added.

"What does that have to do with anything?" Walt asked.

"The murder of his son, like I was saying as you were both there anyways his son never agreed with him and would not help him destroy you or your grandfather." the, Prime Minister said looking to Walt. "He hopes this new apprentice will do as he asks to help him achieve what his son would not!" the Prime Minister said taking a breath.

"Who is this new apprentice?" Walt asked becoming confused again.

"The son of a blacksmith sir, I have not found out the name yet. That is what I plan to do in the coming days" the Prime Minister said bowing to them as he prepared to leave.

"Thank you Prime Minister for your help if that is all you are dismissed." Elza replied allowing him to leave.

"Thank you both for your time, I will do anything that I can to help stop this war and plan to report back as soon as I find anything." he said giving them both another bow and a small smile. He was then escorted out of the throne room by a guard.

"We are now much closer to the end of this war." Walt said smiling at Elza once they were alone.

Chapter 6
Siegfried and Mondomour

The walls of Mondomour's castle were lined with red and black upholstery and sparkled as the morning sun came in through an open window. Voices could be heard in one of the towers of the castle. "Siegfried I am honored you chose to join me" Mondomour said grinning at the little boy standing before him.

"You promised me that you wouldn't hurt anyone." Siegfried replied looking scared.

"Oh dear boy what I have planned will change the world I assure you. Hurting people is one of my littlest intentions!" Mondomour making his lie sound as honest as possible. "Now how about I take you out to the city so that you can test out your abilities?" Mondomour asked waiting for a reply from Siegfried.

"I want to go home and let my father teach me instead of you. The reason why you're being so nice to me is because you want me to help you kill my friends!" Siegfried said narrowing his eyes at Mondomour.

"That isn't true I may have been mean or as you say it "evil!" But please I swear I've changed!" Mondomour said pleadingly.

"I won't believe you, now as I was saying I'm going home and I'm never ever going to help you!" Siegfried shouted at Mondomour. He drew his wand and ran from the castle without turning back. Mondomour didn't bother stopping him instead he decided to take out the next stage of his plan but not before trying one last time to persuade the little boy to trust him and become his apprentice.

"Fine if that boy won't help me then I will just do things alone that way I won't have any problems but I won't give up hope for a new apprentice just yet." Mondomour said to himself as he came down the tower steps. He saw Siegfried running back to the city his legs carrying him as fast as they could. Mondomour ran to the castles open gate and began to slowly rise into the air. He flew as high as he could so that Siegfried wouldn't see him toward the boy's house. Soon Mondomour landed in front of Siegfried's front door and waited for him.

"What are you doing here?" Siegfried said coming to his house out of breath. "Go away! I've already told you..." Siegfried said but Mondomour interrupted him.

"You want power don't you Siegfried?" Mondomour asked him smiling slyly. Siegfried looked at Mondomour with gleaming eyes.

"Well yeah but not if I have to hurt my friends to get it." Siegfried replied narrowing his eyes again at Mondomour.

"Not to worry your friends will not be hurt, just let me teach you magic that even your father could not master" Mondomour replied a grin coming to his face. "With my help you could become the next king of England and soon everyone will listen to you." Mondomour said smiling down at Siegfried. "Just agree to become my apprentice and everything you ask will soon become yours." Mondomour said giving Siegfried a moment to think.

"Ok I'll do it," he replied smiling at Mondomour. "Great now let me begin your training." Mondomour said happily. They went back to Mondomour's castle and went straight to the dungeons to begin Siegfried's training.

"Now your first step to becoming my apprentice is to make sure you know the basic spells and curses." Mondomour said drawing his wand and waiting for Siegfried to do the same. "Repeat after me *Levitato!*" Mondomour said pointing his wand at a stool in the corner of the room. Siegfried repeated with success. "Nicely done, now try this while pointing your wand at your body" Mondomour directing his wand to the center of his chest. *"Rasisio!"* he said rising into the air. Siegfried repeated it and soon he felt his feet leave the ground.

"Wow!" he said happily looking to Mondomour.

"How do I get down?" Siegfried asked frightened that he would be stuck there hovering forever.

"Oh you just raise your hands a little and you will gradually come back to the floor," Mondomour said looking up at him. He did as Mondomour instructed and then once he was safely back on the ground they decided to stop for now.

"Excellent work for today, we will continue again tomorrow then I will show you how to perform things without the aid of your wand. You are free to go. " Mondomour said smiling again at Siegfried. Siegfried left the dungeon thanking Mondomour and heading back toward home.

Chapter 7
Merlin's Final Words

Merlin paced the castle tower in confusion he was in the middle of working on a very important document that would be given to Walt later that day. He came back to his desk where the parchment was laying and took the quill from the bottle of ink. He knew it would be a lot easier to use a pen, but he preferred to do things the old way. There was a knock on the door and he rose from his chair. The door opened and Sophea entered looking frantic. "Oh Sophea nice to see you dear." he said looking at her smiling.

"Great grandpa do you know where Siegfried is? I haven't seen him all day?" Sophea said making an angry face looking up at her great grandfather.

"I'm sorry dear I haven't seen him either. Sorry, I will tell him you were looking for him if I do see him okay." Merlin replied.

"Tell him it's rude to keep a princess waiting!" Sophea said raising her eyebrows at Merlin heading out the door and down the stairs.

"Okay I will." he said going back to his work laughing to himself. Sophea came down the tower steps and began walking through the corridors of the castle towards the outer gate. She then rounded the corner of the castle to the backyard of the castle. She saw her father feeding Ickaris and ran to him.

"Daddy have you seen Siegfried I've been looking for him all day?" Sophea said looking up at her father.

"No sorry honey I haven't." he said turning to her smiling.

"Well can you please help me look for him?" she asked pleadingly.

"Sorry honey I am really busy today, I wish I could but I have a lot to worry about." Walt said looking down at his daughter sadly.

"Okay fine!" Sophea replied with frustration in her voice. "Can I help you feed Ickaris then?" she asked.

"All right." he replied happily. Then Sophea grabbed a piece of pumpkin and reached it toward Ickaris. He licked her little hand and she giggled happily. Merlin came walking out to Walt handing him the piece of parchment he had been working on earlier. "What's this?" he asked giving Merlin a questioning look.

"My will" Merlin replied looking Walt right in the eyes. "Are you serious?" Walt asked flabbergasted. "You really want me to take this?" Walt said still confused.

"Walt you know that I won't be around forever, and so I wrote out my will." Merlin said quietly to Walt so that Sophea wouldn't hear him.

"But shouldn't you give this to my father?" Walt asked.

"Yes, However you are king so I thought since I am here anyway I should show you first" Merlin said holding the piece of parchment out to his grandson. They stood talking for a while then went in for supper. Walt decided to go to the city after supper to talk with the people about his plans to continue fighting. He finished his supper and then headed out for London on the back of Ickaris. Soon he landed the people crowded around him, reporters and camera crews squeezed through the people and tried their best to get as close as they could to the king.

"I have come today to tell all of you that my wife and I have spoken to the Prime Minister and we have come up with a plan to eliminate the enemy." Walt said lying for the first time as king.

"How do you expect to do that your highness?" asked one of the reporters pointing his microphone at Walt.

"We have not discussed exactly how or when we will work out our plan but I assure you not to worry this is my problem and I plan to take care of it as soon as I can." Walt replied trying his best to look honest. Walt then got back on Ickaris and flew back to the castle. He arrived minutes later and walked into the entrance hall. Elza came running towards him.

"Walt hurry it's your grandfather he just collapsed in the armory!" she said sobbing grabbing his hand. Walt and Elza then ran through the castle into the armory and Walt stopped in the middle of the room. He fell to his knees and held his grandfather in his arms and began sobbing.

Chapter 8
A Night of Bloodshed

"Attention all of England the queen and I have decided to finish what was started eight years ago on this day I call to all who are willing. Come to the castle tonight to prepare for battle!" Walt said as he spoke into the microphones" that were placed around him. He and Elza had decided to keep the public out of the castle courtyard for now because of what happened earlier that evening. They were instead speaking to their people via television. "My grandfather has suffered terribly because of the enemy even now he lies on his death bed as I stand before you" Walt said holding back the tears. "All those who wish to end this war and bring peace back to our nation join me and help me fight until the enemy is vanquished!" Walt said looking into the camera trying to keep his wits about him. Then the camera crew shut all of the equipment off leaving the castle thanking and bowing to Walt and Elza. Walt then turned to Elza hugging her as he prepared to leave after assembling those of whom would join him.

"I love you. You know that!" Walt said looking into her eyes. She started to sob and he hugged her again. "I will be back I promise be and strong take care of Sophea while I'm away tell her to be a good princess. Tell her she means the world to me." Walt said softly.

"I will I promise, I love you!" Elza replied releasing his hands. Then he bent down looked at his daughter who had tears in her eyes.

"Daddy has to go now, but before I do you have to promise me to be a good girl while I'm away." Walt said holding tightly onto his daughters tiny hands.

"I promise I will. Daddy please bring Siegfried back safely." Sophea replied hugging her father tightly.

"Know that you and your mother will always have my love no matter how far away I might be." Walt told her whispering softly in her ear.

"I promise to bring Siegfried back to the city safely no matter how far or hard I have to look to find him." Walt added letting go of his daughter standing back up. He gave each of them one last kiss climbed onto Ickaris's back and was just about to leave for the city to gather the others when Sophea called out.

"Daddy wait your going to need this!" Sophea said giving him one last smile handing him Excalibur. He sheathed it gave his daughter a smile then flew towards the city as fast as lightning. He flew low over the city to let the people know that now was the time to follow him into battle. Thousands of men came rushing from their houses giving their children and wives one last goodbye following Walt and Ickaris toward Mondomour's castle. Soon they neared the castle. Walt motioned for the men to fan out and surround the castle just before he flew straight into the castle smashing out one of its walls.

"WHERE ARE YOU!" he yelled as he jumped from Ickaris's "Show yourself you coward!" he said lowering his voice again. Walt ran through the castle until he came face to face with Mondomour. He then grabbed his throat throwing him to the ground forcefully. "What have you done to my grandfather?" Walt screamed at him with anger on his face.

Walt held his wand to Mondomour's throat while still squeezing it with his other hand. "Tell me!" Walt demanded clenching his teeth.

"You'll never get a word out of me" Mondomour said gasping while still managing to smile at Walt evilly. Walt suddenly felt the tip of a wand poke the back of his head and he spun around. Siegfried was standing behind him his arm outstretched with his wand pointing directly at Walt.

"Get away from my master!" He said narrowing his eyes angrily. Walt knew that Siegfried was being controlled he looked back at Mondomour glaring.

"What did you do to him?"

"There is nothing you can do to save him now he belongs to me. *Evica Lomorum*," Mondomour said and Walt quickly dove out of the way hitting Siegfried on accident which caused him to be thrown against the wall the boy crumpled to the floor unconscious.

"You always believed you could beat me but I'm afraid every king no matter how foolish or courageous has to die sooner or later." Said Mondomour who was now back to his feet. "I'm afraid young Walter that your time is now don't worry I will take care of your family." Mondomour said smiling at him. Mondomour withdrew his wand and aimed it at Walt. "Goodbye you disgraceful, morbid creature!" Mondomour said narrowing his eyes at Walt.

"You have caused my friends and my family too much grief and so now Mondomour you will die for it!" Walt replied grabbing the hilt of Excalibur.

"So a sword fight is what you want do you?" Mondomour asked not intending to give Walt the chance to answer. "I to have a sword although mine does not have a legend behind it." Mondomour replied looking enviously at Excalibur.

"I have not come to fight you I only want to know why you've done what you did. If you will not tell me I'll send this sword straight through your heart," Walt said gripping Excalibur so tightly his knuckles were turning white and he could feel the roughness of the hilt digging into his flesh.

"I Walt plan to keep my reasons to myself, if you feel that you must kill me than go right ahead. But know this I shall return to only continue my quest of your throne and to kill everyone throughout the city and your precious royal family!" Mondomour said putting both hands to his sides waiting to be killed. Walt ran at Mondomour with his sword aimed right at him.

"You will be the only one to die tonight!" he said loudly his words echoing throughout the room. Excalibur went straight into Mondomour's heart and

Walt could see his life leave his eyes. "You will never return ever again!" He yelled as Mondomour took his last breath. Mondomour felt his body go cold, his knees buckled and he collapsed to the floor. Walt quickly pulled his sword from Mondomour's body and grabbed Siegfried who was still out cold. He called Ickaris and flew out the window. Before flying away from the crumbling castle Walt withdrew his wand from his pocket and pointed it at the building once he was a far enough distance away. *"Oblivia!"* Walt shouted and a green line of sparks shot out of the end of his wand hitting the castle causing it to fall and crumble to the ground. Walt then took Siegfried back to the castle and went to see his grandfather. Walt entered the tower quietly and slowly walked up to Merlin's bed.

"Ah you're back what happened to Mondomour?" Merlin asked weakly.

"Mondomour is dead I killed him and blew up his castle, he won't hurt us anymore." Walt replied softly. "What did he do to you anyway?" Walt asked. Merlin hesitated then spoke.

"He used his dark magic through my thoughts" Merlin said looking to Walt with a smirk.

"What do you mean your thoughts I had no idea that was possible!" Walt said confused.

"Walt in order to use the type of dark magic Mondomour used on me he did everything he could. He knew what to do to prefect it." Merlin replied sounding better now. "He knew that by making us believe he was weak he could force his way into my thoughts with his magic and kill me" Merlin said sadness coming to his eyes.

"But grandfather I don't see how his magic combined with your thoughts could and almost did successfully kill you?" Walt asked his head beginning to hurt because of all the confusion. "I mean why couldn't you stop it?" Walt added.

"Magic like that should've killed me but I realized once I knew what he was doing and I was beginning to weaken that I could try to stop him. So I began to force the magic out by thinking good things, it turns out before I was able to succeed the thoughts of death that I had in my head were his key to allowing his dark magic to grow within me thus weakening me up to this point." Merlin said giving his grandson a thankful and loving glance. "If it wasn't for you telling me my crazy thoughts needed to stop. I would most likely be dead right now." Merlin finished smiling at Walt. Walt stood staring suspiciously across the room.

"What is it?" Merlin asked him.

"I guess I just don't understand how every time we kill him he always manages to come back?" Walt replied looking again to his grandfather. Merlin took a long breath and then spoke.

"The reason is because Mondomour was given his father's magic just before his father was killed by King Arthur. Mondomour's father Zamfodour was pierced in the heart by that sword you have around your waist." Merlin said looking to Excalibur then to his grandson and continuing. "So Zamfodour cast a spell that sacrificed himself for his son. Then before he was stabbed he transferred his magic to Mondomour, then he became weak and the blade was able to kill him." Merlin said worry on his face. Walt looked shockingly at his grandfather then found his words.

"So you mean Mondomour gained his father's magic and then became afraid because he didn't have anyone to help him. So he fled in fear leaving his father's body?" Walt asked.

"Exactly Walter I'm afraid you have brought the boy Mondomour passed his magic to right into your castle." Merlin said giving Walt a nervous look. Walt's mouth fell open as he fainted.

Chapter 9
Mondomour's Heir

"The Prime Minister is here, Your Majesty," a guard said coming into the entrance hall bowing to Elza.

"Send him in." Elza said pacing the entrance hall. Then the guard left to get the Prime Minister.

"Hello your highness." The Prime Minister said coming toward her and bowing. "I have come in regards to your husband's actions."The Prime Minister said sitting down on a coach opposite the queen. Elza breathed heavily speaking after a moment of silence.

"I am aware of the trouble he may have caused but I assure you he had to do it otherwise he would be dead!" Elza replied in her husband's defense.

"I understand what could've happened but that does not mean he can continually go after this wizard and kill him without consequence. Action has to be taken however, I promise he will not face charges yet." the Prime Minister replied folding his hands.

"What charges? We rule here my husband will not be thrown out of power just because he has been trying his hardest to keep this country safe. He has broken no law!" Elza said raising her eyebrows and becoming angry.

"Your majesty you are forgetting that the action of murdering someone is a crime and if I may I would like to add that there are some who are deeply outraged due to recent events." the Prime Minister said fighting back.

"The only ones who are outraged by this are those of Mondomour's army who have been trying to push my husband and I out of power ever since we became king and queen, we are in the middle of a war and if your angry because of what has taken place I hate to say it but death is a part of all wars!" Elza replied becoming outraged. "Whose side are you on anyway? A few days ago you came here and spoke to both my husband and I about how we would put an end to this war and stop everything once and for all. Now you're telling me we could go to prison against our will for what has occurred that is preposterous!" Elza said coming to her feet at last.

"Your highness it is my decision to do this, all I'm trying to say is that this fighting and killing must come to an end!" the Prime Minister said also now on his feet.

"On whose authority is it that commands this? As queen my husband as king and you as Prime Minister "Who else assumes that they have control?" "We do not promote violence or therefore death as we have previously discussed I believe we all want the same thing!" Elza said calming a little.

"It is by command of the Wizard League madam that a restraining order and suspension of power will be placed upon you and your husband if things are not resolved. They specifically said that any murder that is to occur from this day fourth that is by penalty of law a specific violation of England itself." The Prime Minister said reading from a piece of parchment he had pulled from his pocket. Elza's mouth fell open and once again she became furious.

"I demand to speak with whoever controls this group!" Elza said giving the Prime Minister an angry look.

"Your majesty I understand that all this is frustrating but I assure you that keeping murders and whatever else may happen in the next few days under control is the least of your problems!" The Prime Minister said taking a seat again.

"What do you mean?" Elza asked looking confused.

"What you do not understand is that with Mondomour once again dead he has supposedly passed on his powers to a certain boy your daughter happens to be quite close too," the Prime Minister said giving Elza a worried look.

"Are you saying that Siegfried the blacksmiths son who is but a five year old has acquired Mondomour's power?" Elza asked shocked.

"Yes your majesty and I'm afraid that if the boy is to remain here he will have to be placed somewhere far away from your daughter." the Prime Minister replied shaking his head.

"But what do you have in mind sir?" she asked turning as white as a ghost.

"I will do all I can to keep everything from getting out of hand, if I can I will try my best to speak with the Wizard League representatives' and also talk with General Tumzil to see what he recommends" the Prime Minister said getting up again. "For now I'd advise you and your husband to talk about keeping things here under control and be sure to keep your daughter as far away from the boy as possible." Since I have no magic power I do not know how much help I will be when trying to speak with the W.L. but I will try as best I can to work things in your favor." he said smiling at Elza.

"Thank you Prime Minster, I'm sorry for getting angry at you it is not your fault. You are dismissed." Elza said getting up as well and shaking hands with the Prime Minister. Then he gave a bow and rushed from the castle as quickly as he could.

"Mommy why did Siegfried go with Mondomour and try to kill daddy?" Sophea said as she came around the corner. Elza had a look of horror on her face as she saw her daughter coming towards her. She was afraid that Sophea had heard everything.

"Come here?" she said reaching out to her daughter. Sophea came and sat her on her mother's lap looking intently up into her eyes.

"Honey Siegfried didn't know what Mondomour was capable of, so he thought Mondomour was trying to help us and agreed to join with him." Elza said trying to make things as easy to understand as she could.

"But mommy I don't want him to kill daddy, he is my friend and he would never hurt people I care about." Sophea cried sadly.

"Sophea I don't want you to worry Mondomour is gone and Siegfried will be okay." Elza said calmly as she hugged her daughter close to her. "Your father and I are doing what we can to bring him back to normal." she added holding back tears. "Siegfried will be okay and he will always be your friend." she finished taking a deep breath.

"I don't believe you, if he were my friend he would have left the bad man when he had the chance." She said holding tightly to her mother.

Chapter 10
A New King for Mondomour

"My brother is dead! I leave for a few months and that stupid king kills my brother!" Uvelda said very upset.

"Uvelda I know you're disappointed but Mondomour passed his powers to one of Walt's companions." Goldor the goblin said overhearing Uvelda as she stormed into the castle.

"Who is it?" Uvelda asked looking at the goblin with a grin coming to her face.

"A young boy called Siegfried the blacksmiths son." the goblin replied not knowing how to react to Uvelda's thoughts. Uvelda stood and thought a moment with an angry look coming to her face.

"You mean my brother passed his powers to a five year old?" Uvelda asked her anger rising.

"I believe so your evilness." Goldor replied cowering in fear of the witch before him.

"I want that boy locked up and my brother resurrected and power restored to my family!" Uvelda commanded yelling at the goblin.

"But mistress the boy is at the castle of the king and if we just go barging in we'll be thrown in the dungeons." Goldor replied looking back at Uvelda with fear in his eyes.

"I'm not that stupid Goldor, I unlike you make my plans then wait for the right moment to attack." Uvelda said calmly once again. Suddenly the castle doors were blasted open and Siegfried quickly strode in to where Uvelda and Goldor were standing.

"I come with a direct command from your brother." Siegfried said staring up at the witch. Uvelda stood laughing looking back at Siegfried.

"My brother as you know is dead, so I no longer fall to his commands. Especially if they're from a five year old such as you." Uvelda said regaining her composure.

"Then he told me to do this" Siegfried said raising his wand.

"Oh my boy but I too have a wand and if you..." Uvelda said suddenly stopping as she was beginning to float into the air.

"*Ascendo*" Siegfried replied casting Uvelda higher and higher into the air with his wand.

"PUT ME DOWN YOU UGLY LITTLE BRAT!" Uvelda screamed at the top of her lungs looking threateningly at Siegfried.

Goldor ran in horror for fear that he would be next if he would stay within a few inches of the boy. "*Flameo Ascendo!*" Siegfried said as he put away his wand and caused a flame to go straight at Uvelda using his hands. Uvelda began to fill the corridors of the castle with screams of pain as the flame swallowed her and began burning her flesh. Siegfried suddenly put out the flame as he slowly closed his hands. Then Uvelda plummeted to the floor with a crash. "Now leave this castle and give me control of Mondomour's army or you too will be sent to the grave!" Siegfried said eying Uvelda who was charred very badly from the flame.

"You can have whatever you want just don't hurt me!" Uvelda pleaded looking up at Siegfried from the floor.

"You must also promise to leave the royal family alone!" Siegfried commanded.

"I'll do anything you ask just let me live." Uvelda begged getting up and bowing to him.

"Have my father brought here and have kings clothes made for me" Siegfried said pointing his wand at Uvelda threateningly. Uvelda sent Goldor into the city to get Siegfried's father while she began work on Siegfried new clothes which were going to be fit for a king. Soon Goldor returned with Siegfried's father and ran over to Uvelda to help with the boy's clothes.

"Son, what are you doing?" Siegfried's father asked looking to his son.

"I'm becoming a king daddy." he said smiling at him evilly. Then Uvelda quickly drew her wand aiming it at both Siegfried and his father.

"*Imobulum!*" Uvelda screamed at them causing them to freeze in place unable to take action. "Goldor quickly take them to the dungeon and lock them up. I'm going to bring my brother back once and for all!" Uvelda said running quickly from the castle disappearing. Goldor quickly grabbed the two of them and went to the dungeons while Uvelda went off to her brother's castle in search of Mondomour's remains.

Chapter 11
Mondomour's Daughter

Uvelda came closer and closer to the smoldering mound (This is my brother's castle?) she thought eying it with a sense of pride thankful for not losing her own. She scanned the area searching for her brother's body turning her head from side to side. Then as she walked around the area she noticed someone standing far off in the distance and began to make her way toward the person . As she got closer Uvelda noticed that the person was a young girl around the age of sixteen. She had long blonde hair and she wore a long hooded blue colored robe and was standing right over what Uvelda noticed to be Mondomour's body. "Who are you and why are you here?" She asked the girl as she reached her. The girl said nothing she just stood looking sadly at Mondomour's body. "Who are you?" Uvelda asked again.

"Did you do this?" the girl finally said looking to Uvelda sadly.

"I had nothing to do with my own brother's death, why would you think such a thing?" Uvelda retorted back at her aghast. "Why would you think such a thing?" she added quickly.

"It wouldn't be the first time you tried to cover something up with lies." the girl replied smirking and narrowing her dark green eyes at Uvelda.

"Who are you to call me a liar?" Uvelda snapped back at her. "I have proof that the king himself did this!" Uvelda said looking at the mangled heap that was her brother.

"I can't believe you don't even remember your own niece." the girl replied ignoring Uvelda. "My name which you probably can't remember either is Mena I am the long lost daughter of Mondomour and you Uvelda are my aunt." Mena added turning away from her.

"Oh my God it is you!" Uvelda said coming towards Mena.

"Stay away from me!" Mena said forcefully while drawing her wand. "I don't follow my father's evil ways like you do!" She said pointing her wand at Uvelda's middle. "My father killed Tom my brother, for that he deserves he deserves whatever he becomes." she said looking angrily at her father's dead body.

"How can you say that he's your father, he loved you, he told me so." Uvelda replied lying giving Mena a look of shame.

"My father only cared for one person and that person was himself and no one else." Mena retorted back starting to walk away.

"Where have you been all this time?" Uvelda asked changing the subject while trying to act motherly even though she never really cared for either of her brother's children.

"I was in..." Mena began then stopped. "Oh why does it matter to you my father never cared about me anyways!" Mena said going even further away this time at a faster pace. "I toured Europe alone for awhile." she said calling out to her aunt even though she knew that she wasn't listening. "I'm leaving now and if you follow me I'll have you arrested." she called out as she pointed her wand into the air and disappeared. Moments later she appeared in Merlin's tower. "Merlin! I must speak with you." Mena said. Merlin turned and shrieked at the sight of Mena.

"What are you doing here?"he said eyeing her suspiciously.

"Merlin I'm Mondomour's daughter Mena, I came seeking help." Mena replied smiling at him.

"I know who you are it's just shocking to see you here, I thought you were dead!" Merlin replied raising his eyebrows.

"I've come to tell you that my father isn't dead." Mena said looking down sadly.

"How do you know this?" Merlin asked.

"I have powers that allow me to sense his presence and also tell when he is close." Mena replied looking back up into Merlin's face. "I know he is alive because I see it." Mena said pausing. Then she suddenly froze and her eyes rolled into the back of her head. Merlin stared in horror seeing only the whites of the young girl's eyes.

"Tell me what you see?" Merlin said to her wondering if she could hear him.

"He is coming close he does not have his body back yet but my aunt is trying to revive him. She paused for a moment then started again. "He is planning to take over the city and kill everyone tonight!" she said then was silent once again. Merlin couldn't believe what he was seeing or hearing! "Is there anymore?" Merlin asked her waiting for a response.

"Yes!" she continued. "My father is planning to send a message to every dark wizard and witch throughout the entire United Kingdom. "she said concentrating on her father's thoughts.

"When?" Merlin asked with horror in his voice! Mena then came out of the trance and her eyes rolled back to how they should be.

"I'm sorry Merlin I have to go!" Mena said sounding as if he were in trouble. "I am in danger!" she added.

"What? But what about the message?" he asked becoming even more nervous, "When will it happen?" he asked looking frantically around his tower.

"My father kept that from me, now he knows I'm back, he's coming to kill me and take the country!" she said hurriedly! "I must hurry good luck Merlin." she said kissing him on the cheek and raising her wand into the air.

"I will return one day I promise." Mena said disappearing at last and leaving Merlin standing alone in his tower once again.

Chapter 12
A Message in the Sky

The army made single file lines outside of the castle, Walt and Elza had made plans with the Prime Minister to eliminate Mondomour's dark army.

"We are here today to put an end to this raging battle and stop Mondomour once and for all as your General I plan to take action and to do whatever it takes to stop this evil from spreading!" General Tumzil said loudly. The Prime Minister spoke soon after General Tumzil he showed the men and women where they needed to go in order to attack and remain safe at the same time. Walt and Elza took Sophea and flew away to where Mondomour's castle had once stood Merlin soon went after them. They arrived there to see that the castle had been completely restored and Mondomour waiting for them on a tower balcony.

"Hello your majesties oh and Merlin surprised to see me?" Mondomour stood smirking at them. Merlin my daughter's presence was detected in your tower just this morning. Can you explain why that was? Walt and Elza looked at Merlin suspiciously. Sophea was oblivious to what was going on as she stood holding her mother's hand tightly. What does he mean his daughter?" Walt finally said.

"I thought Tom was his only child." Merlin stood staring right at Mondomour. Then he slowly raised his wand. "I'm sorry I never mentioned anything to you two," Merlin said still keeping his eyes glued to Mondomour. "Mondomour has a daughter, her name is Mena." Merlin said to them hoping that they would forgive him for keeping her a secret for so this long.

"Yes he kept a secret from his family and to think my daughter is trying to help all of you!" General Tumzil and the army appeared behind Elza, Walt, Merlin and Sophea stood aiming their wands at Mondomour. "Look at you all who have come to try and kill me. Come to me my followers it's time to put an end to the royal family, all the others that follow them." Mondomour said raising his hands into the air and smiling at everyone evilly. Mondomour's dark army of Minions came out of the sky and soon lightning and thunder echoed throughout the sky. "Kill them all, don't stop until every one of them is dead!"

Mondomour yelled to his army who were now preparing to fight Walt's army and royal guards. "Leave the king to me!" he added. Rain started to fall and sparks flew and hit many people. Walt held Elza's hand tightly. "No matter what happens I love you both and I always will!" he said kissing both of them.

"I love you too daddy but please don't fight him!" Sophia pleaded. "I don't want to lose you!"

He clutched his daughter's hand, "you won't I promise." He then called Ickaris and jumped onto his back. He flew to the highest tower of Mondomour's castle. Mondomour was following him and slashing at him with his sword. They both landed on the top tower. Walt drew Excalibur.

"You will die for good tonight, I assume you know the ways of sword fighting or is dark magic your only purpose?" Walt questioned.

"Dear Walter you know had I not learned the ways of sword play I wouldn't have a sword now would I"?

"Then as king of all England I challenge you Mondomour Lord of Darkness to a battle to the death!" Walt exclaimed.

They put the blades of their swords together and the fight began. As the swords hit sparks showered down around them. Walt felt the vibrations of Excalibur go from its hilt up into his arm as Mondomour's sword clashed against his blade.

"Face it you are done for now, you have no medallion to save you!" Mondomour laughed.

"Hand over your crown and my rightful place upon the throne!" he exclaimed.

"I will never lose to you and you will never be king" Walt screamed!

"I cannot die you know that you may try to kill me but each time that you do you will fail!" "I will be here whether you like it or not!" Mondomour yelled. Slashing at him with all of his strength.

"If you want me dead you will have to do better than that!" said Walt. Walt was trying to hold back the blade of Mondomour's sword. Walt grabbed his wand from the inside pocket of his robe with his free hand. He still held onto Excalibur as tightly as he could.

"Oblivia!" Walt screamed and Mondomour fell off of Walt and flew over the tower's edge and hit the ground with a thud. Walt got up from the tower's floor and walked over to the tower's edge and looked down and saw Mondomour's mangled body. Then he sheathed Excalibur and called Ickaris. He flew down to where Elza and Sophia were standing.

"It's time to go home! This fight is over!" Walt exclaimed. "Merlin get all of these people back with their families.

"Understood, Sir," Merlin replied looking to his grandson happily.

"Daddy what is that?" Sophea said looking up at the sky. Walt and Elza looked up and saw these words in the sky: I shall return you haven't seen the last of me! They knew those were the words of Mondomour. Walt looked over to where Monodomour's body had been and noticed that it was gone.

"Let's go home now." Walt said tiredly and they flew towards their castle.

Chapter 13
The Loss of a Loved One

The battle was over but the cries of pain and loss continued. Many were wounded and numerous graves had to be dug.

"I don't believe what the General and the Prime Minister said was right." Elza said looking to Walt with frustration on her face.

"What do you mean?" Walt asked her as they soared through the air on Ickaris's back.

"So many died and we stood back like we thought it was right we achieved nothing but hate." Elza replied with sadness in her voice.

"Elza you and I are doing the best we can. If you think things should be changed go to Parliament and fight for what you believe to be right. Remember whatever you decide to do I'll always be there standing beside you. If you go down I won't be afraid to fall with you." he said compassionately stroking her cheek and looking into her big blue eyes. "The Prime Minister has told us that he went to the Wizard League and came to an agreement which said that we would not go to prison for any reason no matter how things turned out as a result of war remember?" Walt added turning back to look ahead and keep an eye on the skies. "We have to stop Mondomour now and I believe the longer we ignore things the worse they'll get. " Walt said as the wind came up. "If we don't stand and fight Mondomour will think he has won and try to take England. But if we stand up to him and fight he'll realize he won't get what he wants so easily." Walt said as he came in for a landing in the courtyard of the castle.

"Walt I just don't want anyone else to die and I'm afraid that if we continue to ask them for help they'll just turn against us." Elza said as she slid down from Ickaris's back and walked into the castle. Upon entering a nurse ran toward them crying.

"Y-your m-majesties it's Merlin he's gone!" the nurse sobbed as she motioned for them to follow her to the tower.

"Mommy, daddy!" "great grandpa just collapsed when he was teaching me." Sophea said running to her parents. She started to cry as they picked her up and held her. Walt slowly walked over to Merlin's bedside and stared in horror as he saw his grandfather lying dead and white faced on the bed. He slowly put his hand on his grandfather's forehead and smoothed his white hair back as tears came to his eyes and felt the icy coldness that radiated through his grandfather now. He held his wife and daughter close as they came to him and hugged him standing over Merlin crying.

"Call my parents now, my father needs to know." Walt said wiping his eyes and turning back to the nurse who still was sobbing uncontrollably. She bowed to him wiped her nose and quickly turned from the room. Walt, Elza and Sophea stayed up in Merlin's tower crying into the night.

"Funeral arrangements will be made for tomorrow." Walt said holding back the rest of his tears. Then they covered his body with a sheet and finally let him go in peace

Chapter 14
Ending the War

Walt's parents came to the castle later that evening both his mother and father were in shock as they saw Merlin's body. Walt's father could hear sobbing all throughout the castle.

"I'm going after him Elza and I'm not coming home until he's taken care of!" Walt said as he prepared to leave to fight Mondomour once again.

"But why you'll only get hurt. Elza said pleading with him not to go.

"He's taken too much from us, I want you to send Sophea with my parents and announce to the city that the war is over." Walt said looking into her eyes deeply then hugging her.

"You want me to lie to them!" Elza said looking up at him as if she couldn't believe what she had just heard. "I'm sorry but that I cannot do, not now not ever!" she said furiously back at him. Walt then turned from Elza looking sadly at her and then walked out to where Ickaris was kept. He smiled at his dragon and unhitched the chain that was around his neck and climbed onto his back.

"All right Ickaris to Mondomour's castle." Walt said giving the dragon a soft pat. Ickaris began to run and as soon as his big feet left the ground he started to flap his wings. Within minutes he and Walt were soaring high above the castle. As they flew Walt was filled with the thoughts of what had happened between him and Elza. It angered him that she wouldn't do as he had instructed. He also understood her reasons for not wanting too. They soon came to the castle as soon as Walt was within a few feet from the ground he jumped from Ickaris's back and stormed through the castles doors. "Mondomour show yourself! I have come to avenge the great Merlin my grandfather!" Walt called out loudly as he looked around the castle for Mondomour. The candles flickered all throughout the castle when soon a cloud of black smoke appeared in front of Walt. It began to take the shape of Mondomour and Walt drew his wand.

"That will do nothing to me." Mondomour said.

"Magic is strong enough to do anything even kill the most evil of beings!" Walt replied aiming his wand threateningly at the smoky figure of Mondomour.

"Tonight is the night where you will die just as your foolish grandfather did." Mondomour said materializing into his human form. He withdrew his wand from the pocket of his robe and pointed it at Walt. "I suppose to make it fair I'll play your way." Mondomour said smiling evilly at Walt.

"Now before I spill your blood tell me what is your reason for coming here?" Mondomour said to him although he already knew.

"Keeping us from battle only angers me more. But I have come to avenge my grandfather, to keep the country and my family from any further harm." Walt replied through gritted teeth. Mondomour walked around Walt eying him suspiciously then after a few minutes of silence he spoke.

"You are a noble king, but to be honest you are not the one I am after. I already killed the one I was after." Mondomour said grinning more broadly and taking a breath. "Unfortunately Merlin would still be here now if it hadn't been for his foolishness, if he had only given me that medallion." Mondomour said eyeing the medallion at Walt's neck. Walt then drew Excalibur and slashed at Mondomour but Mondomour was quicker and waved his wand. Suddenly Walt was thrown across the room and hit the floor with a thud. "Soon I will take your place as the rightful king of England and all the people will praise me for being much stronger than you." Mondomour said as he walked slowly over to where Walt was lying. He laughed looking down at Walt then kicked him hard in the ribs. He then slowly rose his wand and pointed it at Walt. "I hope you enjoy death more than I have." Mondomour said. "Oh and don't worry about your family they'll be in good hands." he said getting ready to kill Walt. Walt wanted so badly to say something but his injured ribs prevented words from coming. All

Walt wished for now was that he could get help from the only creature that could come to his aid.

"Ickaris" he panted and suddenly Walt heard the dragon's heavy wings beating the air outside the castle. Mondomour stopped in mid sentence and looked around for the source of the noise. Then with a loud bang Ickaris crashed into the side of the castle. He opened his big mouth and a big ball of fire erupted from it. Mondomour was then engulfed in the ball and he began to shriek loudly in pain. Then as quickly as it had begun the enormous flame ball disappeared. Mondomour unsheathed his sword and was about to stab Ickaris when Walt drew his wand and pointed it at Mondomour. *"CONSTRICTO!"* Walt shouted and Mondomour was hit with a green ball of sludge he then hit the castle floor as his wand and sword flew from his hands. Walt saw Ickaris grab the ball of sludge with his claw that now held Mondomour tightly. He then bounded from the castle and out of the city. Walt then stood dazed and confused as to where his dragon was taking Mondomour but he soon ignored it pointed his wand upward and disappeared.

Chapter 15
Farewell to Mage

Walt returned to the castle and was sent directly to the infirmary where he was cleaned up and his wounds were tended. Then he had his grandfather's body prepared to be placed in the royal tomb just outside the castle. Crowds of people lined the streets and music started to play as Merlin's body was moved to the tomb by a carriage pulled by horses. Only those of Merlin's family were allowed to enter the tomb. Once by the tomb Walt waved his wand and the tombs door was moved aside the family went inside. Walt's dad with Walt helping him moved Merlin's casket into one of the many underground vaults that were spread throughout the tomb. Together they lifted the vaults lid and moved it into place as the casket was set inside. Then Walt's father spoke to his family.

"I never would've expected my dad to go like this but seeing as he out lived almost everyone he knew I know he was happy" he said trying his best not to cry. "I thank everyone who could be here today and those who couldn't but wanted to thank you also." Walt's father said finishing his little speech. Then everyone left the tomb in silence. Once back at the castle a feast was prepared in Merlin's honor and everyone in the family sat and enjoyed delicious food and talked about their many stories of Merlin. Once the meal was over everyone said their goodbyes and left. Then Walt and Elza went for a walk in the garden. It is weird without him here." Walt said as he and Elza walked hand in hand through the rows of wonderful smelling flowers.

"It is but you know even the most powerful wizards can't live forever" Elza said sadly.

"If he knew he couldn't live forever then why did he create a medallion that is supposed to keep the person who wears it immortal?" Walt replied with frustration in his voice.

"I'm not going to talk about this with you, besides he wasn't wearing the medallion" Elza said taking a slow breath. She stopped as tears came to her eyes and slowly began to stream down her face. Walt hugged her tightly holding back his own tears and pain. "I just wish he would've had the medallion, then things would be different" she said wiping away her tears. They walked back into the castle as it started getting dark and up into their room. They climbed into bed said good night to each other and went to sleep hoping that tomorrow would be a better day.

Chapter 16
Sophea and the Witch

The dungeon was flooded with light from the morning sun, Siegfried and his father sat wondering how they possibly could escape the tiny cell they had been thrown into. They had been held in the dungeons of Uvelda's castle for what seemed like months. "Dad when are we going to get out of here?" Siegfried asked looking at his father sadly.

Siegfried I don't know I hope it's soon though" he replied looking back at his son hopefully. There was a noise above them and they heard it coming closer.'

"What's that noise Siegfried asked looking to his father again with a scared look on his face.

"Siegfried quiet they'll hear you!" his father replied in a hushed voice. The noise came even closer and now the sound of running could be heard. Suddenly they heard a door squeak open and a shadow reflected off the stairs leading to the rooms above.

"I'm here to help you" said a girl's voice. Soon Mena was in the dungeons looking at Siegfried and his father. "I'm Mena Mondomour's daughter, I'm here to rescue you" Mena said looking back at their smiling faces. "I have your wands right here." she said reaching into her robe pocket and pulling out a long black wand and a long silver wand handing them to Siegfried and his father. "I'm not sure if you know this or not but before my aunt left she destroyed a lot of things and part of the stairs so just be careful when you go up them" Mena said unlocking the cage with a key. Then they all very carefully made their way up the stairs and into the room above. "You two go back to the city. I have to look around a bit to see if my father has stored anything here that might help us destroy him" she said looking around for any objects that may look like they are enchanted. The two then ran for the castle doors until they were outside. Then they grabbed hands rose their wands and disappeared. Mena looked for what seemed like hours failing to find anything useful. She searched every inch of her aunt's castle in the hopes that she would find what kept her father from dying. With no luck she headed for the city. Soon she entered the city and rushed for the castle gates. "I must speak with the king about stopping my father" Mena said to the guard standing outside the gate nearly out of breath.

"The king is busy, he doesn't want visitors today" the guard replied. Mena could sense a lying tone in the guard's voice but she ignored it.

"All right" she said walking away. She couldn't convince the guard to let her in so she only had two people left that she could talk to, those people were Walt's parents. She then held up her wand and disappeared. She arrived at Walt's parent's house and took a deep breath knocking on the door. She waited a few minutes and soon Walt's father answered the door. He looked Mena up and down and smiled at her.

"What is it?" he asked.

"I must talk to your son but the guard at the castle won't let me in. It's about stopping my father" Mena replied giving Walt's dad a hopeful look.

"I'm sure we can come up with something to convince him to let you in" Walt's father said smiling at her and stepping outside. They then disappeared back to the castle gate. They appeared at a distance from the gate and walked the rest of the way back up to the guard.

"Hello there I believe that this girl has some news for my son" Walt's father said to the guard who stared blankly back at him.

"The king is busy training his daughter" the guard replied.

"I'm sure he would gladly take a break from that especially to hear some news about Mondomour" Walt's father said giving the guard a shameful look.

"All right go in if the king is upset don't come running to me" the guard said giving in and pushing open the gate. They found Elza coming in from the royal gardens and she directed them to the dungeon where Walt was training Sophea.

"Now Sophea show me *Imobulum*" Walt said to his daughter as he stood watching her. Mena and Walt's father waited until she was finished casting the spell before speaking with Walt.

"Son Mena has told me that she has some news about Mondomour and she wishes to speak with you about it" Walt's father said looking to his son urgently!" "I'll leave you two to it then" he finished going back up the dungeon stairs.

"Sir I know your busy but I think I know why you're unable to stop my father every time you try" Mena said looking up at him. "I think he has something similar to your medallion but I'm unsure" Mena said with a sigh.

"Well how do you know for sure?" Walt asked.

"Well I have the ability to sense my father's presence when his is alive and also hear his thoughts" Mena replied.

"So what makes you think he has something that keeps him alive just as I do?" Walt asked looking at Mena confused. "I heard him talking to my aunt just before I returned and hat is why I chose to come back" Mena said hoping the king believed her.

"What do you mean you heard them were they talking about whatever it is that keeps him alive or how do you know?" Walt asked her again more confusion coming to him.

"Like I said I have the ability to not only sense my father's presence but also have the power to look into his thoughts" Mena said pausing for a moment and then continuing. "I can sometimes see where he is and what he is doing at the same time." Mena said catching her breath.

"Okay you heard them talking then and also, saw it do you know where this supposed object might be?" Walt asked looking at her happily.

"No sir only that something exists and I'm afraid without it being destroyed or even knowing what it may be we have nothing against him."

Mena replied looking down sadly.

"Well thank you for the help I think if I look into it more we might get somewhere." Walt said smiling at her.

"Pardon me sir but I couldn't help but notice you training your daughter. I happen to know a lot about increasing and enhancing the power of certain forms of magic and if you wouldn't mind I would be glad to stand in on a few lessons with her and evaluate her spell casting ability." Mena said to Walt as he began to turn away.

"Oh well yes that would be wonderful if you would help in making my daughter a better spell caster." Walt replied turning back to her and smiling happily. Then Walt went back to his daughter and motioned for Mena to come speak with them.

"Sophea this is Mena she has told me that she can help you become better with the spells I teach you. I have agreed to let her stand in on a few of our lessons and then she will take notes and later help you prefect the skills you learn" Walt said looking down at his daughter.

"But daddy I want you to teach me I don't want two teachers" Sophea said whining back at him.

"Oh but she won't be here for all of our lessons just until you are strong and can perform magic without assistance." Walt replied.

"Okay fine I'll let her help." Sophea said looking down at the floor sadly.

"All right good, to start with show me *Imobulum* again" Mena said smiling at her. Sophea then pointed her wand at a suit of armor standing across the room.

"*Imobulum!*" Sophea said and suddenly the suit of armor stood straight in a saluting pose.

"Excellent that was brilliant!" Mena said smiling at her. "That is all I need for today, I will be back after your next lesson to continue evaluation until your able to show me that you can perform and use magic unattended" Mena said to her still smiling. Then Sophea walked from the dungeon and back to her room. Once alone Walt spoke.

"I think she'll become very good with a wand in time" he said looking to Mena and smiling. "I also want you to know that I'm not a killer I don't thrive on the thought of killing your father, I just am trying to get him to realize that people who murder others for no reason need to and will be punished!" Walt said hoping she would understand.

"I know sir." Mena replied smirking a little to him. Then they left the dungeon and Mena went out into the city alone.

Chapter 17
Losing Power

It had been days since the battle, Ickaris continued flying until he at last reached Greenland. Mondomour was clutched in the dragon's claw, he had not moved and it was as though he were dead. Within his chest his heart beat slowly, his eyes were crusted shut and his flesh was badly burned. He looked like a skeleton, he was even paler now than he had been before and it was as if all his blood had been drained from his body. Ickaris landed on a cliff that was entirely frozen over with ice and placed Mondomour aside. He then stood on his hind legs and widened his wings. Then they began to shrink, his blue scales became a velvet cloak and his head, hands and feet became human. It had been decades since he had been in this form. He looked at Mondomour and grabbed his arm. "You have tortured to many and now you shall be punished," the human Ickaris said. He then stuck out his hand and placed it on the icy cliff face. It began to melt away and form a hole, soon it was big enough for a human to fit inside. Ickaris then threw Mondomour inside glaring at him. "May God have mercy on your soul!" Ickaris said just before sealing the hole. Then Ickaris transformed back into his dragon form and flew back home to the castle.

Chapter 18
A Hidden Legend

Ickaris returned home and was taken back behind the castle where he slept. Inside the castle Sophea had decided to look at the many books in the library. She would get a book flip through it, maybe read a few words then put it back. She had been going down an aisle near the back eyeing the shelves when a book with a purple cover and red writing caught her eye. She pulled it from its place in the shelf to read the title. It was titled: Legends of Old England, Sophea decided to ask her father to read it to her and held it close to her and left the library in search of her father. She had searched everywhere and finally found him in his bedroom staring out the window.

"Daddy can you read this book to me?" Sophea asked walking into the room to her father. Walt turned to his daughter and she handed him the book. He took one look at the book and looked back at his daughter.

"Where did you find this?" he asked sitting on the bed looking at her.

"In the library is it a bad book?" she asked him frowning.

"Oh no I was just curious," Walt replied opening the book.

He flipped through the book until he came to the middle where he saw a picture of a dragon that was unusually similar to Ickaris. The title of the story was called: The Legend of Ickaristhe Master of Elements. Walt decided that he would read this story to Sophea partly because it was short and partly because he wanted to know what it was about. "A long time ago there lived a man called Ickaris he had the power to control every element in the world." Walt paused and looked at the picture again beginning to wonder.

"Why did you stop reading?" Sophea asked as she sat on her father's lap looking up at him.

"Sorry," he replied then he continued. "As time went on people began to become jealous of his extraordinary powers. Ickaris knew that if he didn't find some way to hide he would either be killed or locked up, so he went to an alchemist he knew would be glad to help him. The alchemist's name was Phineas Loch who was a man with a love for the skill of potion making. So Ickaris went to him asking him to help him hide." Walt took a breath and thought more about what he was reading. He continued before noticing he had stopped. "So Phineas gave him a potion that he had said would allow him to transform into a dragon. Once a dragon he was told he must be put in an egg just like a baby dragon so he agreed to let the alchemist seal him in an egg. Once it was done Phineas acted as if it were a real dragon egg that he had placed up for sale. Then years passed and the egg was purchased by a young man. Ickaris was never seen again" Walt said finishing the story and closing the book. Sophea then took the book from her father returning it to the library leaving him alone again in his bedroom. Walt couldn't help but wonder if that legend were true or not and if it were true how had he not known. After all the picture he had seen resembled his dragon almost exactly. He needed answers even if he were wrong. The only problem was he didn't know who to go. The only person who probably would've known was dead so the only thing he could do now was wonder

Chapter 19
Mondomour's Lifeline

Uvelda appeared in the doorway of Mondomour's castle. She had been absent during her brother's battle with the king so she was unaware that he was not there.

Mondomour where are you? It's your sister" Uvelda said into the silence.

"My father is gone he was taken by the king's dragon after their battle," Mena replied as she appeared in the hallway.

Uvelda jumped as she saw her. "Where was he taken?" Uvelda asked giving Mena a questioning look. "How do you know they had a battle?" she added. Mena drew her wand.

"I have the power to see things with my mind you know" Mena replied with an obvious look on her face. "I have a question for you and if you don't tell me what I want to hear you'll suffer the consequence of death" Mena said pointing her wand at her aunt ready to strike. "Where is my father's power source hidden and what does it look like?" she asked threateningly.

"You honestly think that I'm going to tell you?" Uvelda replied laughing. Uvelda eyed her niece very closely then continued. "I'd rather die than tell you where the location of my brother's life is" Uvelda said narrowing her eyes evilly.

"So be it!" Mena replied raising her wand. "*Evica Lomorum!*" she screamed and the curse flew right at Uvelda who braced herself against the floor. She held up her hands as the spell came nearer holding the curse back with all the dark magic she had.

"You want your father's source of life yet your willing to kill to get it" Uvelda said as the curse vaporized with a crack as it came in contact with her dark magic. Then Uvelda straightened up smirking at the girl. "All right seeing as you're not trying to kill him and you are his daughter I will show you" Uvelda said going up a staircase with Mena following close behind. Uvelda then stopped almost pushing Mena backwards.

"You must first tell me where my brother is or I will not show you where his life source is" Uvelda said coming to the top of the stairs at last. Mena concentrated her mind on finding the location of her father soon her eyes rolled into the back of her head.

"I see that he is inside a mountain in an ice like cavern. He is nearly ice himself but his heart still beats" Mena said pausing and taking a breath.

"Where! Tell me where!" Uvelda pleaded. Mena continued.

"The location is too hard for me to identify, all I know is that he is enclosed in an icy cavern somewhere in the world" Mena replied finally coming back to normal. Then she withdrew a knife from inside her robe pocket and dangling it for Uvelda to see.

"Now tell me where to find his life source otherwise I will cut your throat" Mena said with anger on her face and in her voice. Uvelda then motioned for Mena to follow her when they came to a long hallway. Then they came to another staircase and began climbing the stairs.

"Up here there is a passage" Uvelda said coming to the top walking briskly towards what looked like a dead end. "Your father's life source is concealed within a dark ball of magic" Uvelda said stopping at the wall.

"What is this mysterious thing concealed within the magic ball?" Mena asked stopping behind her aunt.

"My dear this thing that contains your father's life is something that even Merlin himself would never have dreamed of" Uvelda replied raising her eyebrows. She then withdrew her wand and pointed it at the wall giving it a wave. The wall suddenly formed into a doorway within it another staircase that led upwards. Uvelda walked up the stairs Mena following her at a quick pace. Inside the room it was dark and candles lined the walls. At the far end of the room a faint purple glow could be seen coming from a sphere shaped container. "Over here" Uvelda called from across the room and Mena quickly walked to where her aunt was standing. Mena looked in amazement at the purple shining sphere and saw a tiny fairy fluttering inside of it. She started to wonder why her father would allow such a tiny creature to be the keeper of his life.

"Why a fairy?" Mena asked keeping her eyes on the tiny creature. "How do you remove it? I mean it was placed in the sphere so it could be removed right?" Mena added looking toward her aunt. Uvelda stared at Mena aghast but speaking anyways.

"So many questions, I'm sorry to tell you this but if we were to remove the fairy your father would slowly die just as the fairy would." Uvelda said looking at her niece with a confused look. Mena began to wonder if there was another way to destroy the orb and save the fairy but she kept these thoughts to herself so that her aunt wouldn't catch on to her plan. Mena would tell the king as soon as she could get away from her aunt but for now she stood looking in amazement at the tiny creature.

Chapter 20
Betrayal

"What do you mean?" Elza asked Walt as she finished reading the story he had read to Sophea. "So what your telling me is that you think your dragon is the person in this legend?" Elza added staring at her husband in disbelief.

"Yes don't you see the dragon in this picture and my dragon look exactly alike and isn't it weird how I named my dragon Ickaris and the man in this legend is named Ickaris too?" Walt replied looking at Elza as they sat on couches in the library. Elza looked at Walt then back at the picture in the book.

"Okay I do admit it does seem a bit weird but it's probably just a coincidence." Elza said closing the book.

"But it is all right there, how can you say that it is just a coincidence? when I'm almost positive that we could have someone right outside that could help us defeat Mondomour" Walt replied staring at Elza with anger in his eyes.

"Are you accusing me of calling you a liar?" Elza asked looking at Walt annoyed by his attitude. "Honestly all you ever talk about or care about is fighting a stupid war with one of your grandfather's old enemies. You never take time to be alone with me or your daughter" Elza said pushing away from Walt and leaving the library. Walt clenched his fists and rose from the coach going after his wife. He caught up with her and stopped her.

"Don't you ever say that to me again you know that's not true. I do everything I can to make you both happy!" Walt said angrily to Elza. "Mondomour may have started this by taking things out on my grandfather but as long as I live I will never let him take out his hatred for him on the rest of us" Walt said calming a bit.

"That's it I don't want to do this but I'm afraid that if I stay here any longer it will drive me insane. I'm not going to get mad at you I just don't know what to believe so I'm taking Sophea and we're going to my parents for a few days until you can learn to control your temper and end this war once and for all" Elza said going up to get her daughter from her room. She returned carrying her bags in one hand and Sophea in the other. They left without another word and silence filled the castle. Walt stood alone in the entrance hall with the book of legends clutched in his hands looking down at it regretfully. He hated when Elza left him, so he decided that he had to prove to her that he was right and show her that he cared for her and Sophea. He had decided he needed some rest in order to get his mind off of what had happened. But then as he was about to go up into his bedroom the castle doors were flung open. Walt spun on his heels and saw a cloaked figure coming toward him. He quickly drew Excalibur and held it out in front of him bravely.

"Who are you? How did you get in here?" Walt commanded quickly.

"Do not be alarmed I have come to help you" the cloaked figure said.

"Who sent you?" Walt asked trying not to let his fear show. "Your grandfather Walter" the cloaked figure replied. Walt froze for a moment then spoke, "How do you know my name?" Walt asked becoming even more afraid.

"I have known more than just your name for many years your highness" the cloaked figure said lowering his hood. He then pointed at the book Walt still held in his hands. Walt quickly flipped to the story of the alchemist and the dragon and saw a picture of a man. He then looked back at the man before him and noticed that the two matched each other exactly.

"Ickaris is that you?" Walt exclaimed his eyes nearly popped out of his head.

"I was beginning to wonder if you'd ever figure it out," Ickaris said smiling. Walt was speechless as he stood eying Ickaris in amazement. While his mind was spinning with many questions. "You mean all this time you've been human without anyone knowing?" Walt asked looking at Ickaris finally seeing him for who he truly was.

"Not exactly human I am more human than I am creature but not human entirely," Ickaris replied showing Walt his hands and ears. His ears were pointed like an elves and his fingers had claw like nails on them. "Look here at my teeth, notice how they are fanglike he said opening his mouth a little. Walt shook his head as he looked with more amazement at Ickaris's shiny teeth.

"So is the legend true about the alchemist and all the rest?' Walt looked at Ickaris questionably. Ickaris wondered why he was being asked such an obvious question but he let this pass and spoke.

"If it weren't true I wouldn't be standing here before you now would I?" Ickaris replied smiling proudly. Walt knew he was foolish for asking that question but for all he knew the legend could have been altered by someone.

"My wife left and I need your help to bring her back here," Walt pleaded to Ickaris. Ickaris immediately transformed into his dragon form and Walt climbed onto his back. Then they flew from the castle as quickly as they could. Soon they landed in the yard of Elza's parent's new cottage which they had moved into shortly after Walt and Elza took the positions of king and queen. Then Walt jumped from Ickaris's back and ran up to the front door. He rang the doorbell and soon Elza's mother answered the door.

"Oh I see you have come to talk with my daughter," she said smiling at him. "Come in," she said looking out at Ickaris who sat waiting out in the yard. Walt entered the house and ascended the staircase to the guest room where Elza was.

"I came to apologize and ask you to come home," Walt said entering the room and looking at his wife who sat on the edge of the bed. Elza turned toward him and spoke softly.

"No I'm the one who needs to apologize, I know you care about Sophea and I very much I was just getting angry about the war and what Mondomour has done," she said hugging him. Suddenly a scream erupted from the lower level of the house both Walt and Elza jumped running from the room and down the staircase. Mondomour lunged at Walt knocking him to the floor. Elza screamed and ran for her daughter who was curled up unconscious against the wall.

I have come to get what is rightfully mine," Mondomour said demanding the medallion. "Your little plan didn't work Walter," Mondomour said as he stood over Walt pressing his foot against his face. "Your little dragon tried to trap me in an icy grave in Greenland. Until recently I was helped to freedom by a so called friend of yours. I believe his name was Edward Hucklesbey no need to worry once he helped me I murdered him then fed his body to the loch-ness monster," Mondomour said laughing.

There was a loud crack and Mena appeared in the room holding the fairy that held her father's life in her hands.

Chapter 21
A Fight for Freedom

"I would stop now if I were you," Mena said as she looked into her father's eyes with anger. The fairy was struggling against Mena's forceful grip trying its best to get free.

"How the bloody hell did you get that?" Mondomour asked looking at his daughter fearfully.

"Aunt Uvelda showed me where it was kept, then as she left I found out how to retrieve it from the magic orb you kept it in," Mena replied smiling proudly at him.

"Please Mena as your father I beg you return it to its case!" Mondomour said looking at her like a lost puppy. Mena could sense the fear in her father's voice.

"Your Majesties I have here in my hand the link to my father's life. It has been removed from the orb that keeps it alive and thus it will slowly die out along with my father" Mena said turning to show Walt and Elza. Walt was now back on his feet and alongside Elza and their daughter who was still out cold in her mother's arms.

"Mondomour I declare you under arrest for the murder and torture of various people of this country. You shall be imprisoned for your crimes until your last breath!" Walt commanded. Mondomour slowly put his wand away and he was then escorted back to the castle dungeon to live out the remaining days of his life. It was then that both Walt and Elza realized that they had won the war.

Chapter 22
A Dark Days End

"We must announce to the city that the war is over, and also that Mondomour is in prison" Walt said to Elza as he came up from the castle dungeon.

"We've told our people that too many times, I highly doubt that they will believe us this time without actual proof," Elza replied turning to her husband. Walt knew that Elza was right but the only problem was he had no idea how he could convince everyone in the city that the war was over and that Mondomour was slowly dying in the castle dungeon.

"Is Sophea all right?" Walt asked.

"Yes she's sleeping now," Elza said looking to him and smiling. Walt then decided that now would be a good time to show Elza Ickaris's human form.

"Come with me there is someone I want you to meet," Walt said holding out his hand to her. Elza eyed him suspiciously but took his hand and walked outside in wonder anyway. "Now I know this might be shocking I didn't believe it at first either," Walt said as they walked together behind the castle. They came to where Ickaris was kept and Walt looked deeply into his eyes. Then Ickaris began to transform. Elza watched in amazement until Ickaris was completely transformed.

"How is this possible I can't believe this. It can't be," Elza said as her mouth fell open. Walt smiled at her in her state of shock. "Like I tried to tell you before it's in the book his story," Walt said looking to Ickaris and smiling proudly at him.

"It is an honor my queen to finally be able to show you my true form," Ickaris said bowing to her. "I have told Walter that I would be honored to help you both in destroying Mondomour," he added giving Elza another smile. They both smiled at Ickaris then Elza spoke.

"We thank you for your kindness and are very honored to have you with us," Elza said giving Ickaris a slight bow. Ickaris followed them into the dungeons once inside he and Walt went to the dungeons.

"What are you doing here get out of my face!" Mondomour said to Walt as he saw him enter. He then took notice of Ickaris and stepped back in horror to a corner of his cell. "Y-you what are you doing here?" Mondomour asked staring in horror at the man next to Walt.

"I have been with Walt even before he heard your name I was given to him by his grandfather and was from then on his sworn protector," Ickaris replied giving Mondomour a menacing look. Mondomour was speechless, he stood frozen with fear staring at the two of them on the other side of the cage. How was he supposed to win a battle against someone he knew little about. Let alone survive without his life source in its rightful place.

"You may think you have won and I may not be at my strongest but remember I always manage to find a way back," Mondomour said weakly. Walt laughed at Mondomour's words.

"You honestly think you can come back?" Walt questioned staring in disbelief at his enemy. "If I'm not mistaken your father believed the same thing. But he didn't make it to far now did he," Walt said smirking at Mondomour. Mondomour lunged at Walt but before he could get to him Ickaris held out his hand and a yellow ball of electricity shot out of it hitting Mondomour right in the center of his chest. He was thrown backward his head hit the back of the cell and he crumpled to the floor.

"You're turning into your father Mondomour, personally I expected better of you," Ickaris said mockingly as he took one last look at Mondomour and followed Walt out of the dungeon. Later that evening Walt and Elza announced the news of Mondomour's capture to the people of England. They received lots of cheering and applause not expecting such a joyous crowd. Afterward Walt went to find Mena to try and persuade her to destroy the fairy.

"As much of a threat that my father is to the country, and to your family I cannot just end his life," Mena said to Walt as he entered her father's castle. Walt's heart filled with anger.

"What do you mean?" Walt said looking at Mena bewildered. "Your father has killed more than enough people and I won't stand for it any longer!" Walt said angrily.

"I understand you're angry even though he has killed many innocent people that does not mean he deserves the same fate," Mena replied in her father's defense realizing that this was the first time in her entire life that she actually stood up for her father. Mena's eyes filled with tears. "I will not become a murderer as evil as my father is I have no choice I am his daughter and I love him," Mena said beginning to sob. "If you were in the same position and your daughter had to decide to either kill you or keep you alive I'm sure she would do as I am doing," Mena said becoming silent once again. Walt stood silent for a moment then spoke.

"What have you done with the fairy?" he asked looking around for it.

"I put it back where it belongs," Mena replied wiping away her tears. Walt was about to run out of the castle when Mena held him there.

"You know Tom would do the same thing," she said looking sadly at the king. Walt hated having to remember Tom, every time he did his mind would drift back to the memory of the day he was killed. Mena then let her hand fall back to her side as she stood watching him go from Mondomour's castle.

Chapter 23
Destruction of Darkness

D ay's passed and still no change took place throughout the city. Everyone including Walt and Elza were beginning to lose hope in ever seeing the country free of darkness and the threat of Mondomour. Ickaris remained his human form and began taking the place of Walt as Sophea's teacher. He taught her about the elements and the past. He was on constant watch for anyone wanting to threaten the royal family and also was the new guardian of the medallion. Siegfried was beginning to be able to control the magic that was transferred to him from Mondomour and he was also using it for good instead of evil. His father was busier than ever making weapons and armor for almost every family in the city. Mena had been true to her word and had taken the fairy and placed it in a little ball of magic which she hung around her neck, in her spare time she would go see her father who remained in his cell in the castle dungeon. "I want you to take this, seeing as it is rightfully yours," she said to her father one evening while visiting him. She then took the fairy from her neck and handed it to him

"Thank you unlike your brother you understand what taking England means to me and I admire that in you," Mondomour said taking the fairy from her and kissing her hand softly. She smiled back at him and left the dungeon without another word. Later that evening Mondomour sat and thought about various ways he could escape and recover his wand and sword which were someplace in the castle. He then realized he had the power to shape shift. He couldn't believe he had forgotten then he slowly closed his eyes and began to think of a mouse. Suddenly he felt himself beginning to shrink. Soon he had become a tiny grey mouse and he crawled from his cage. Then out of nowhere he heard footsteps coming down the stairs. Sophea came running after a ball she had dropped while trying to make it levitate with her wand. Mondomour froze but it was too late Sophea had already seen him. She extended her hand quickly grabbing him before he had a chance to escape. He struggled against her grip but was unable to get free. She ran back up the stairs and straight to Ickaris and held Mondomour out to him.

"You never learn do you?" Ickaris said staring at the tiny mouse with pity. He stuck out his hand and the mouse changed back into Mondomour who was now sprawled out on the stone floor. Then before Mondomour could react Ickaris quickly took the fairy from his neck.

"Give that back you have no right taking that from me!" Mondomour commanded now on his feet. Ickaris held it high in the air as Mondomour tried to jump for it and failed with each attempt. Ickaris then quickly ran to Walt who was in the throne room. Mondomour shrank back down to the floor in fear realizing that if he should try to run he wouldn't get far without his wand or sword to aid him. So he stayed on the floor once again rather than being captured or worse killed. His time had run out, he had lost everything and at any moment he would die but would face death with open arms.

Chapter 24
One Last Battle

Mondomour rose from the floor minutes later and slowly walked toward the throne room. He came around the corner and saw Walt on his throne. Envy filled him but another part of him from deep inside told him that he was doing the right thing. He continued toward the throne and Walt saw him and waited until he was directly in front of him to speak. "Ickaris here tells me you have escaped yet again but don't worry I know what you're here for," Walt said calmly looking into the eyes of his enemy. Then Mondomour looked up and spoke.

"You are not my enemy your grandfather was I took every bit of it out on you because of some stupid artifact." Mondomour said sadly. He paused for a moment to take a breath then continued. "He was my best friend long ago before we became enemies. It changed once he began to help the king. He began to spend little time with me and Arthur became his number one priority, soon the only time I would see him was when he was up in his tower working on something for Arthur." He paused again holding back tears and then spoke as his heart pounded very fast within his chest. "I soon found out that it was the medallion you now possess, then very soon after Arthur was crowned king I came across a fairy and began testing out various ways that it could keep me immortal" he finished his story keeping his eyes on Walt. Then Walt stood and told Ickaris to give him the medallion. Ickaris obeyed taking the medallion from his neck and placing it in the king's hand. Walt then slipped it over his head and came down the landing to where Mondomour stood.

"Thank you for that story Mondomour, however you must be executed," Walt said looking at him sternly. "Instead of you going straight to your death I have decided to make it more fair and fight as a real king should through a battle to the death," Walt said taking a long breath. Mondomour looked surprised but tried his best not to show it and Walt continued. "You take your fairy and I will take my medallion and whoever pierces the other's first wins," Walt said doing his best to avoid the look on everyone's faces. Elza stood coming toward him but Ickaris stopped her.

"NOOO! I WON'T ALLOW IT!" she screamed as tears came to her eyes.

"Silence!" Walt said coming toward her and taking her into his arms as she sobbed. "It is the only way to end this war," Walt replied hugging her. Then Walt and Mondomour stepped out into the center of the room, they both drew their swords and began to fight. With each clash of their blades sparks and ringing filled the air. Elza, Ickaris, Sophea and Mena stood watching in horror as the two fought. Then within the blink of an eye Excalibur went straight into Mondomour's heart, his blood spilled everywhere and the fairy at his neck slowly quit fluttering. With his last breath Mondomour held his sword up and plunged it into the medallion and through Walt's chest. Then Mondomour fell before the king dead.

"NOOOOO!" Elza screamed as Walt fell to the floor weakly. She ran for her husband and held him in her arms crying. She knelt close to him with Sophea at her side tears falling from their eyes. Elza pulled the sword from Walt as gently as she could watching his life leave him. "Don't leave me, oh God don't leave me" she sobbed kissing him.

"I...I will never leave you," Walt said through labored breaths. "I guess heroes have to die sometime" he said his eyes slowly closing.

"I love you and only you, remember that," Elza replied sniffling kissing him one last time.

"S...Sophea you are my little princess and I love you...never forget that" he said looking at his daughter and kissing her.

"Daddy I don't want you to go!" Sophea cried to him.

"I..I must I will see you again someday.. I love you both and always will" Walt said closing his eyes. He then lay motionless as his wife and daughter cried over his body on the cold stone floor.

Epilogue
Fifty Years Pass

It had been many years since the day England lost its king, now queen Sophea ruled. Her mother perished due to natural causes and she was buried alongside Walt. Evil no longer threatened the country, it seemed as though with the passing of Mondomour evil left as well. Ickaris had left the city soon after Elza's death, he hadn't left because of the terrible things that had happened but because he knew that if he would stay in London evil would soon return. The medallion had been buried with Walt, it's power lost with him. With everything that became of the heroes of the past England seemed to remain unchanged as well.

About the Author

Tait Ressler lives in Bismarck, North Dakota where he has enjoyed writing stories for much of his life. He enjoys reading many books of Fiction that involve lots of adventure, mystery and magic. When he isn't writing or reading he enjoys spending time with his family and friends. Tait began writing in the eighth grade as a hobby and has loved it ever since, he wishes to continue writing many more stories and hopes to one day move overseas to England.

LaVergne, TN USA
24 February 2010

174022LV00001B/2/P